American Retired Spy

By

Donald R Richter

DORRANCE PUBLISHING CO
EST. 1920
PITTSBURGH, PENNSYLVANIA 15238

Dorrance Publishing Co
585 Alpha Drive
Pittsburgh, PA 15238
Visit our website at www.dorrancebookstore.com

ISBN: 979-8-88729-433-9
eISBN: 979-8-88729-933-4

Chapter One: Hawaii

Mark Neal stepped onto a plane headed for Hawaii, he was flying first class he took his seat, and slid his briefcase under the seat. The woman next to him, was around forty dressed in business casual, she was very cute with her blouse unbuttoned maybe one to many, she sported a wedding ring around three carats she asked, "Are you traveling alone?" Mark smiled and said, "I am on a fact finding mission, I am looking for a nice place to retire, somewhere I can just drop off the map and never be found again." She blushed and said, "You're way too young to retire."

Mark smiled as he settled in and said, "You're never to young, you just have to figure out when you have enough money, and I think I have enough." She said, "You must have a lot because Hawaii is not cheap." Mark smiled and said, "Now that all depends, which island, and how you want to live, the house is an investment, so I did some figuring if I spent a hundred grand a year I would run out of money when I hit seventy-four, then I will be too old to do anything anyway, I could sell the house and move back to the mainland, go into a senior citizens apartment."

He pulled out a book and started to read it while everyone else boarded, it was a five-hour flight. The woman said, "Well it sounds like you have researched it, how much are houses going for." Mark looked at her and smiled and said, "We are not going to talk all the way there are we, and it depends on what Island, the big island I can buy a small house for a quarter million, and a condo for the same price. I was looking for an investment property and something quiet, so around eight hundred grand, I think I will rent for the first year and see if I like the place, it is cheaper the San Francisco, but I do love that city."

She asked, "Where are you living now, and what book are you reading?" Mark smiled and said, "I am living in New York right now so it is going to be a bit more to live but not much, I could live in Mississippi it is the cheapest state to live in, that is what I have heard, you can get a house for just over a hundred grand, I looked at a few online, just like South Dakota, I would rather spend a little more and live-in paradise." She smiled and asked, "What does your wife say?" Mark said, "I am buying the house first, making sure it is in my name before I get married, I have seen too many guys lose everything in a divorce." She asked, "Your thinking of divorce before you even get married?" Mark smiled and said, "This is a process, first I get settled then I am going to find a wife." She asked, "So you do you have a girlfriend?"

Mark asked, "What part of process don't you get? I did the college thing, made a career got enough money to pay off college and retire, now I am ready to kick back and enjoy life and I should be able to finish this book and get a little nap before we land, the book is Fairies Sorcery and the Greek Gods, I read the first book on a different flight Fairies Sorcery and the Devil, and on the way back to the mainland I am going to read Fairies Sorcery and the Titians, the first one sets up the trilogy God gives powers to a guy to wage war on the blue fairy, and to save the red fairies, he brought Merlin into the story and this one he brings in the Greek Gods, you know Zeus and the crew, so what is your story." She smiled and said, "It is a week of sun and sand, at Alani a Disney resort."

Mark asked, "Are you meeting your kids there?" She smiled and said, "Nope just the husband, Disney really knows how to take care of you; we did a couple of Disney cruises before we married and had a great time." Mark asked, "Are you flying up front and him with the cattle?" She laughed "No nothing like that, he is in Chicago leaving tonight doing a redeye, life is busy, the kids are with his mother." Mark said, "Slow down and enjoy, before you know it you will be with kids running to soccer practice, juggling fifteen things at a time." She asked, "Do you have kids?"

Mark smiled and said, "Not that I know of, it's that process I told you about, I still have to find a wife first." She said, "You do know you are doing this wrong, you should find someone, fall in love then find a place to retire." Mark smiled and said, "Nope this is right, I find a place I want to retire buy it so it is mine before getting married, so I get it the way I want it." She asked, "You are thinking divorce again and you are not even married yet don't you trust anyone?" Mark smiled and said, "Well my relationships never lasted long, always chasing the almighty dollar; it's time to settle in somewhere, not on the big island, I have a few properties to look at." A stewardess walked by and asked, them if they wanted anything to drink, the girl asked, for a soft Merlot, Mark ordered a Royal Crown Manhattan.

As the plane was landing in Honolulu, the girl next to Mark said, "Look isn't it beautiful? There is a huge volcano, do you know there are five volcano's here on the big island?" Mark said, "That one is Diamond Head, so you and the hubby have fun on your vacation." She said, "And you keep your eye out for a wife." He lifted an eyebrow and said, "What happens if I am gay?" Her eyes popped wide open then she said, "Well it doesn't matter does it?" He chuckled and said, "Nope not gay, but I could be, actually it would be less drama."

The man across from him said, "You know you would think that, but there is still drama, I could tell you stories, I am sorry I am Josh, I would ask you out for a drink but this is a business trip." Mark said, "Oh I am not staying on this island; I want something a little quieter." The man said, "Well here is my card after you find a place to retire and want to step over onto the other side give me a call, this work thing sucks, the question is how much is enough." Mark took the card and said, "This might sound crazy, but I am going to call you."

The woman said, "Really, you're attracted to him? Boy this is a busy airport." Mark said, "Well he is a good looking guy, I wouldn't say I was attracted to him. I need a life partner, and he would be better than buying a dog, this airport is so busy because not everyone is staying here, this is a connecting flight for a lot of people, that is why it is called a gateway to Asia." Josh said, "Call me in a couple of days maybe I can rearrange things and we can go out for a meal and chat, I like your early retirement idea, we can talk finances."

Mark said, "Yeah I see you're a banker, you do training." Josh said, "We are looking at buying a local bank here, I am the point man, what are you around forty?" Mark reached over and shook his hand, and said, "It would be nice to interview you, and I am going to an island that is private, but I could invite you over, or I could pop over, here is my card." Josh said, "I thought you were retired." Mark said, "I am just haven't made up new cards, what should I put on them- *done working just chilling?*"

The plane landed and Mark got his luggage and hailed a cab, he went a couple of miles and got out at a helicopter pad. He went in a small office and showed the guy his phone which was showing his ticket. The man said, "You do know that is the forbidden island, you need an invite to go there." Mark smiled and said, "Niihau has been in the family of Sinclair/Robinson since 1864, and I have an open invitation, they know I am coming." The pilot said, "Ok I guess we can go then, shall we get your payment and paperwork done? And we will be off then."

They got into the helicopter the pilot fired it up and Mark said, as he pointed, "Your oil pressure is low." The pilot said, "Oh it always is, when it warms up, it will come up." Mark said, "Really, well I sure hope so, these things don't glide long." The pilot reached over and tapped the gauge and it came off the red. He then slowly lifted off the pad and was in the air. Mark pulled out his phone and texted, "Be there in an hour, 666." It was a beautiful day, not a cloud in the sky, as they got close smoke rose from the island, Mark pointed and said, "There, put it on the beach."

The pilot set the copter down nice and easy on the beach, an older couple stood there and watched. Mark got out and opened the rear door and took out his luggage, it was a suitcase a garment bag and a briefcase. He walked a few yards from the helicopter and it took off, he sat down his luggage and held out his hand to the man and said, "It has been a long time; you said, whenever I was in the neighborhood to stop by so here I am." The man said, "James I thought you died." The woman said, "The beast, when are the rest coming?" Mark said, "Oh it is just me; I would like to hang out for a week or so and look at some re-tirement property."

Mark said, "Jinxy my God how did you end up with this old goat?" A sly smile slid across her face as she said, "You didn't call, and it is Keely and Pierce now, so you're going to give up the job." Pierce said, "Good for you old man what are you 45, and it is just you, we received a couple of cases of Bollinger's 2004 vintage, it is a very good may I add." Keely said, "And twenty tins of Beluga Caviar, five different kinds of crackers, a case of Sobieski vodka, six bottles of vermouth and a case of olives, I thought an army was coming."

Mark said, "I didn't know what to send for food I thought we could just eat at the local restaurants, but I noticed there are none." Pierce said, "There is one, not a five star let me tell you, it is laid back here." Mark asked, "Is there somewhere I can change, and give me an hour to decompress on the beach?" Pierce asked, "How long are you planning to stay, would you follow me please?" Mark said, as he picked up his luggage, Keely took his briefcase, "Well I am looking for a retirement home, I need something quiet."

Pierce said, over his shoulder, "You have to talk to the board, each homeowner is on the board, and we just had a house open up on the east side, it's a beautiful place." Keely said, "There are rules, number one is we like it quiet here, and no bringing the job here, do you remember a guy 545, a few guys came to the island looking for him, he was working for the Russians, and a couple of Italians came to talk with him? We disposed of the bodies and cleaned up the place, it was a mess."

Pierce said, "We are here to relax, take it easy, and enjoy life." Mark said, "I can do that and that is my plan, it is nice and quiet here." Keely said, "Tonight you can start talking to the other agents that moved here." Pierce said, "Well this is the house, it is five thousand square feet, four bedroom six baths, we have lighting speed internet, the kitchen is that way, and your room is on the end of this wing we are on the other, there is maid service she comes once a week, so pick up after yourself."

They walked to his room he asked, "So what is the password for the internet?" Keely said, "There is none, we have fiber optic ran to each house, all the electrical is buried, one center generator, 98% of the electricity comes from wind, solar, and the ocean currents, I can't remember the last time the diesel generator ran." Pierce said, "We run it twice a year to make sure it still runs, other than that there are three huge saltwater batteries on the island, so get changed and we will meet you on the deck."

Mark came out on the deck with a Hawaiian shirt and shorts with a cream colored hat. Pierce handed him a glass of champagne and said, "Here is to a couple of weeks of paradise." Keely said, "We used to travel, but now this is home we still go to the Kauai to stock the place." Pierce said, "We have a friend on the island that collects the stuff from Amazon; he makes the trip once a week." Keely said, "We are very environmental here, he has a 50 foot sailboat. They are not the boats of old; one person can sail it."

Pierce said, "We run an electric boat, it has a couple of Tesla batteries so we can make to the island and back on one charge, but we rarely go." Keely smiled as she said, "We keep it plugged in though just in case, it takes a lot of power to push five tons through the water, even though it is a hydroplane." Pierce said, "It is actually a hydrofoil; the whole boat doesn't come out of the water but ninety five percent does. It cuts down on the drag. Come on, let's get you setup on the beach, sit and relax, I will get the bottle of champagne and Keely can start rounding up some landowners, sorry homeowners, you don't own the land, maybe we can tour the 545 house." Mark said, "Whoa, let me get off the hamster wheel for a day, I have to decompress, get rid of some of this jetlag."

Keely said, "I am so glad I don't have to fly around anymore, I must have wasted five years of my life in airports and planes, so here we are our little place to watch the sunset." Pierce walked up with a silver bottle holder and stuck it in the sand. He said, "This is high tec it will keep the bottle at thirty-seven degrees for four hours, we have tested it in ninety-five degrees heat." He turned and walked back to the house. Mark asked Keely, "So how are you two, is the old man good to you?" She stepped up and hugged him then gave him a small kiss on the cheek, and said, "This has been great, Pierce treats me like a queen, you couldn't pay me to go back to work, and the people on the island are fantastic, we have everything we want here. Is it a little expensive to live here? Well yes it is, but we are getting old and don't vacation like we used to."

Mark adjusted the umbrella, and said, "I have to think about this, it is a bit far from civilization, I mean what happens if I want a candy bar?" She said to Pierce "Open the bottle; he needs an hour to clear his mind, now just concentrate on the waves, feel the breeze, smell the orchids." Pierce handed him a glass, he raised his and so did his wife, and said, "A toast, may you find what you are looking for." Mark said, "Aye." Keely took Pierce by the elbow and turned him toward the house and said, "We will give you some time to unwind."

Mark sat under the umbrella sipped champagne, dug his feet in the sand then saw a beam of light out in the distance, and it went straight into space. It shone for a half minute then a burst of light shot up the beam. He sucked down whatever was in his glass he stood and quickly jogged back to the house. He walked in and Pierce said, "Wipe your feet." Mark asked, "Did you see that?" Pierce asked, "What?" Mark said, "I have to call in, a beam of light shot up into the sky, something is going down." Keely said, "How far was it?" Mark thought and said, "It could have been a hundred miles, it was straight out from the beach."

Keely said, "There is nothing out there, come let's look at the footage." Mark asked, "You have security here, I don't see the cameras?" Pierce said, "Well we were going to show you this anyway, follow us." They walked into the back room to a wall which opened up to a staircase and then they went down to a tunnel. Pierce said, "This is an old vent from the volcano, here we are the first room is just data storage." Mark said, "This is huge." Keely said, "I believe it is something like 100,000 petabyte that is like a million terabytes."

Pierce said, "It is big and powerful, but not that big to stand out, now this other room is our security." Keely said, "Every homeowner has access to this we could have used our smart TV to view it." Pierce said, "But we need to be at the source, ok so that was a half hour ago, Alexa show us a half hour ago the view of the ocean to the east." A voice said, "Showing you the view to the east at eight thirty four." Keely asked, "Alexa scan for something out of the ordinary." Alexa said, "Scanning for something out of the ordinary, this is what I have found."

The picture on the screen changed and a beam of yellow light shot up from the sea to the heavens. Pierce said, "Oh my God, it is a satellite killer, Alexa freeze and zoom in to see where that is coming from." The picture of the beam got bigger and a ship started to come into view. Mark said, "A German u-boat, you have to be kidding me." Keely said, "It can't be, those things are antiques." Pierce said, "Show it in slow motion and follow the beam into space."

Mark said, "Look it must have hit something, but why the beam first? Is it to lock onto the satellite?" Pierce said, "Ok Alexa scramble it and forward this to H.Q. and Interpol now." Alexa said, "Encryption started and sending to H.Q. and Interpol." Mark asked, "Won't they track it here, and how is Interpol going to open it?" Keely said, "Nobody will track it here this is a highly advanced computer; it will go through a couple of data farms, and change encryption, and Interpol is a different encryption."

Chapter Two: To Seattle

Mark's watch dinged, he pulled out his phone, as he said, "They don't have my number, and I don't carry the work phone." He put the phone to his ear looked at Pierce and asked, "How fast can you get me to the airport?" Keely said, "Screw them; you're retired." Mark said, "Something is up, and you know I have been working more now than when I was on the job, it is like they don't trust anyone, and I am expendable." Pierce said, "I can get you there in an hour, but we have to shake a leg." Keely said, "I will get the Jeep."

Pierce asked, "How about the jetpack?" She said, "That thing, you want to kill him, that hasn't flown in years, and he has luggage." Pierce asked, "Alexa does 223 still have the rocket sled?" Alexa said, "Searching for rocket sled." Keely said, "No, that thing breaks the speed of sound, we put him on the yacht and put the hammer down and get him there in three hours." Pierce said, "We will have a car waiting for you at the dock, I will call Brandon he has the fastest boat a twenty-eight-foot cigar, he can get you there in fifty minutes."

They hurried back to the house. Pierce looked at his phone and said, "To the beach, you have a copter on route." Keely said, "Henry, he has that little two man thing, this has been a quick visit; you didn't even have time to unpack." Pierce said, "It is a Mosquito; not that fast but it will get you right to the airport, they have cleared you for landing and you have a private jet fueled and sitting on the tarmac, I don't know where you are going, this is coming together very quickly, something is wrong." Mark said, "I know, and why me? I am retired. There are a hundred agents they could use, and that ultra-light helicopter is going to drop in the ocean, it can only carry five gallons of gas, which gives it a range of sixty miles."

Pierce said, "It's a company copter. No, wait, he did the upgrade himself, anyway it is an XE model I believe it holds twenty gallons, and runs on diesel, he figures he can make a round trip with it." Keely's eyes opened wide as she asked, "Has he ever flown to the airport?" Pierce smiled. "No not really, but he has opened it up and has gone over a hundred miles an hour." Looking at his phone, Pierce said, "The XE model does 112 km/h that's around seventy miles an hour, and you're saying this one will do a hundred." Pierce smiled and wrapped his arm around his shoulders and said, "Over a hundred, that is just with one person, nobody likes to ride with him." Mark said, "You have to be kidding me."

Keely smiled and said, "You do know you are one of the best, and you're dead." Mark chuckled and said, "You know what I am, I am disposable. They can use me and throw me away." Pierce said, "That's not it, you are trustworthy, Spectra is running rapid through the agency, we have a hell of a time keeping it off the island."

They got out to the beach to watch the little helicopter land. Mark ran to the lawn chairs and grabbed the bottle of champagne, and he said, "You're right; it is still cold." Keely said, "Give me that, let's get you inside then I will give it back to you." Mark tried to put the luggage behind the seat. It wouldn't fit so he put his briefcase and garment bag back there and climbed into the passenger seat, put on his seatbelt, then Pierce handed him his suitcase. He put it between his legs. Keely reached in and gave him the bottle and yelled, "Be careful." Mark gave the thumbs up sign. Keely took ten quick steps away and the helicopter started to pick speed and took off. Mark looked down to see Pierce and Keely waving. Mark slid on the head set so he could talk to the pilot; he asked, "Do we have clearance to land?"

The pilot said, "Yes we do, they are giving us the right of way, everything will circle until we are down, it's not a big airport anyway, so what was that thing, a big rail gun? Is it a satellite killer?" Mark said, "That is what I think, but they could shoot down the space station, whatever it is we have to find out who is behind it." The pilot said, "I would put money on Spectre, it is getting bigger all the time, you don't know who to trust, by the way I am Sam Smith, and you are 666 the beast."

Mark asked, "So how do you like living on the island Sam or would you rather agent 487? I am Mark Neal, private eye." Sam smiled and said, "Love it, you're going to have to just relax, it will take a month or two to unwind, then it will feel like every day is a Saturday. Are you married?" Mark said, "No." Sam said, "Well one of the rules is no children, and that is strictly enforced, and nothing too noisy, no dirt bikes, unless they are electric. Bob has a couple, I like the golf cart thing I have one with air conditioning, heat stereo, it will do fifty but we don't have any roads that are that flat." Mark said, "This little thing flies nicely."

Sam smiled and said, "I have installed a twin turbo on the diesel, it doesn't look like it is sucking a lot of gas." Mark said, "We are flying at 240 km/h, that is around a 150 mph correct?" Sam said, "That you are; this is the fastest this thing has ever flown, and we are not going to push it, God I am getting old, but when I get it home I want to go over it and make sure nothing is coming loose, this is its maiden voyage with the new motor, ok time to talk to the airport."

Sam said, "Well here we go, I have clearance to land right next to your private jet." Mark said, "Well that's nice the last time they sent for me it was an f-22 Raptor, the service was terrible." The pilot looked over to him and asked, "Really?" Mark nodded and said, "We got to break the sound barrier and everything pushing Mach three, everyone on the mission was expendable, that's when I started to think about finding a place to hide."

Sam said, " Mach three that's over two thousand miles an hour, wow they really wanted you there fast, now if they let you stay, you're going to like the island, it is a piece of paradise, very low key, you should find a wife, or a significant other we have just one gay couple on the island; you remember 951 he is gay." Mark looked at him and said, "No you have to be kidding, really he is gay? I have spent weeks with that guy and he never came onto me."

Sam chuckled and said, "Well maybe you just were not his type, his husband is a great guy, and a great chef, and loves to throw a party, ok I am talking to three people now, I see the plane, and the guide." A man stood waving two orange sticks, ten feet from a small jet. Sam set the helicopter down without a bounce; Mark reached over and shook his hand, then opened the door, swung one leg out letting the suitcase fall on to the tarmac, then reached in and took the bottle of champagne, and behind the seat and grabbed onto his briefcase and garment bag, walked away from the helicopter and tipped up the bottle finishing it.

The helicopter pilot saluted and slowly took off. A young man walked up and said, "Ok you have an emergency flight to Seattle, do you have a rare blood type or something?" Mark said, "It is just a job, I am retired but I guess the management just keeps screwing up, they are paying a big price for me to straighten stuff out, I guess they just don't trust the new guy." The pilot asked, "So what do you do?" Mark smiled and said, "I do a lot of things, mostly corporate takeovers." The pilot said, "Well shall we get going; buckle up it is going to be around six hours."

Mark said, "Great, it seems like I have been living in airplanes, do you have WIFI on this thing?" They got up to cruising height. Mark went into the back of the plane and pulled out his laptop and looked on Google Earth at the island he was just on, there were no roads, it was marked a sanctuary island, no visitors allowed. He looked up the file that was sent to him and studied it, the agent that was working on this case in Los Angeles has disappeared, there was a doctor that was working for the governments secret laser program and is now missing, there was the film of the laser shot and a close up of the ship it was a old U-boat.

He opened a file on the doctor that was working on the laser, he worked out of a secret lab just out of Seattle, and he had a son they lived in San Francisco. He Googled Dr Adam Johnson, a picture came up matching the one in his file, he went to Purdue and was holding a 5.0 GPA all the way through college, he was the top of the class and was an aerospace engineer, in three years. He had credits from ASU, the school of Earth and Space Exploration. His IQ was a 162, Mark looked it up and he fell into the genius category. He holds six patents, four on lasers, one on a fire extinguisher, and one on a rocket powered plane.

There was nothing said about him having a son or ever being married. He closed the laptop and took a nap. The pilot said on the speaker system, "If you would please store everything and buckle up we are coming in for a landing." The pilot sat it down nice and easy, and taxied up to a parking spot on the tarmac. Mark asked, "Do you have a passenger for the ride back?" The pilot said, "It doesn't matter; they paid well to get you here." Mark got off and went to the rent a car; he picked up a small Nissan Sentra.

Mark texted his old boss Thomas back in Chicago, "I need some real information what this is about. I got more about this doctor on the internet then the crap you sent me, something is going on and it is in the system. Where is his work file, what am I doing here?" Thomas sent back, "Someone has scrubbed his file, I am working on getting you a new one, here is his last job he disappeared from, and it is a base up on the Tate creek a secret aerospace lab." Mark drove to downtown Seattle to the Four Seasons, he dropped the car at the valet and showed the girl at the desk his phone she scanned a bar code off of it and said, "Oh you have booked the Governor's suite it is a 2480 square foot room, it has floor to ceiling views of Elliott Bay, Puget sound and the mountain, it sleeps four, who will be joining you?"

She keyed two cards and handed them to him. Mark said, "It is a business trip I am not paying for it. Could I have my bags brought to my room? I am going to catch a meal and a quick drink." Mark flashed her a big smile and said, "Dreary old Seattle, I was just on a black beach in Hawaii soaking up the sun." The bell boy took his luggage up to his room; the man behind the counter asked, "Should I book you a table at the restaurant?" Mark said, "No that is fine, I am going to the Goldfinch to have a snack and a drink, I don't feel like a sit-down meal." The man said, "Whatever you would like, Mister Neal."

Mark walked into the Bar and the bartender said, "Mark Neal long time, the usual?" Mark smiled and said, "Not long enough, that depends; what would you suggest?" The bartender said, "We still have that bottle of Remy Martin Louis XIII." Mark said, "That will be fine, bill it to the Governor's suite." The bartender got out a small step stool and went to the top shelf and took down a beautifully sculptured bottle, he sat it on the bar and gently wiped it off. A woman who was watching over her laptop asked from her table, "So what is so important about that?" Mark said, "It is a thousand dollars a drink, would you like one?"

The bartender asked, "Would you like a cherry and a drop of cherry juice, sir?" Mark said, "Well yes I would if I remember the last one tasted mighty fine and make that two." He took the drinks and handed one to the woman, and said, "Taste and tell me if it is worth a grand." She took it and looked into his eyes and said, "It looks like you were on the beach somewhere, and with fine booze you don't contaminate it with a cherry." Mark smiled as she put the drink to her lips and swirled it in her mouth, she said, "It is nice and soft."

Mark took his second sip and said, "In fact eight hours ago I was sitting on a beach in Hawaii, now take another, the second sip is the best." She took another sip, she rolled her eyes and hummed, then said, "It is so delicate, it has soft notes, a light nutty flavor, and the cherry stands out gives it just a touch of sweetness, this is very nice." Mark raised his glass and said, "Good I am glad you enjoy it." He started to walk away. She asked, "Where are you going, you can't just hand a lady a thousand dollar drink and walk away?" Mark smiled and said, "You have work and so do I, maybe some other day." She took a sip and savored it as she watched him as he walked away in his Hawaiian shirt and shorts; he had a slight limp but a nice pair of legs, still in sandals it looked like he was still on vacation.

Mark sat at a table for two, he raised his hand with a fifty-dollar bill in it, a waiter showed up from nowhere. Mark said, "I would like a salad, I was here not too long ago it had pistachios, pancetta, cherry tomatoes." The waiter said, "That would be the Goldfinch salad." Mark said, "That would be very nice, now I would like that down here first, then I would like the potato gnocchi." The waiter said, "That would be with Lamb Bolognese, oregano, mint and Parmigiano Reggiano." Mark said, "For a main dish I want the New York strip with a side of crispy brussels sprouts, can I have the steak without the fig sauce, or should I have it with?" The waiter said, "That is what makes the dish, most people order extra." Mark smiled and said, "Let's do that then, I will have my salad down here and send my meal to my room, it's the Governor's Suite."

The woman walked over and sat across from him and asked, "Are you eating alone in your room, would you like company?" Mark smiled and said, "They dragged me off of a beautiful black beach, I was having champagne with friends, looking for a place to retire, now I have a huge presentation to pull off and I haven't a clue what to say, you seem to be a very nice girl, and damn good looking any other time, I just have so much to do you understand." She smiled and asked, "So you're married?" Mark said, "No not at all, in fact I was thinking of getting married, but right now I have this thing." She smiled and asked, "So you have a girlfriend." Mark raised a glass and said, "That I do not; I have worked on my career built up a nice nest egg and am ready to settle down." She asked, "Are you going to have children?" Mark smiled and said, "That would have been nice, I am too old for that now, I would be damn near sixty when they get out of school, I suppose I will have to look up some divorced broad."

She took a card from her small designer backpack, she slid it in front of him and said, "When you are done with your business call me, I am based out of New York, but am flexible." Mark smiled and said, "I am sure you are, and I will certainly will." She asked, "Do you have a card?" Mark stood and held out his hand and said, as he took hers gently. "But of course," he pulled out his wallet and went through a few cards and picked one, he gave it to her. She said, "James Barnes, that's not what you said to the bartender, I believe you said you were Mark Neal, and you are in the import export business."

Mark smiled and said, "I do a lot of things and you are very smart; I like that in a girl, here comes my salad, and I never said I was in the import export business, I am a Private Investigator." She said, "Your card says you are in the import export business." Mark smiled and said, "My bad, that is right sorry, but that is my number and e-mail."

He pulled out his glasses and took a picture of her, and as soon as she turned to walk away, Mark said, softly, "I want an in-depth research on this girl her name is Sara Star, she will be going to my James Barnes e-mail, and she will be looking up Mark Neal." His phone rang, he looked at it, a number he did not recognize, he looked at Sara at the other table looking up from her phone. He answered and said, "Ok it is a little weird having two names, Mark Neal is my alter ego, in the investigation business you really don't want people to know who you are, they could track you down and do weird things."

She smiled a large smile as she blushed, then waved, and said, "Just checking, how long are you going to be in town?" Mark said, "This I do not know, but after this job I am retired, then I need to buy a place then get married, do you feel like shopping for a house?" She looked surprised and asked, "Are you asking me to marry you?"

Mark looked shocked, he got up and walked over to her and said, "I don't think so, this is a process, I am going to buy a house get settled, get married, and live a life of peace and tranquility, do you want to travel?" She looked at him and said, "You know, I really don't want to step on another airplane if I don't have to." Mark said, "You are my kind of girl, what do you want to do in retirement?" She smiled and said, "For the first year nothing, I have to catch up on all the stuff I have been putting off, we should get together I have a checklist I want to run by you, so far you have a check in mysterious man, one who works, can I put a check in financially secure?"

Mark said, "How about this, my money is my money, and your money is yours, do you have enough to retire?" She smiled and said, "How much is enough?" Mark smiled and said, "See that is a question only you can answer, how high maintenance are you, do you really have a checklist of what you want in a man?" She rolled her eyes up to look him in the eye and said, "Yes this is a big step, and I have enough, I think." Mark said, "This is not good, I have to focus on the job at hand, now all I can think of is you, have you ever been married, let's skip that, can you e-mail me your list?"

She said, "No silly, this is what I want; you might want something completely different, how long is this meeting or job your working on going to take, you did say you have to make a presentation, didn't you?" Mark said, "Yes I have one hell of a week coming up, I will make myself a note to make a list of what I want in a woman and what I don't want and call you on the 12th and we will see where we are." Sara said, "The 12th, what time?" Mark said, "If I don't call you, then you should call me, now get to work so I can get to mine, so far I like what I see," he turned and walked back to his table.

He turned to see she was still watching him, which was a good sign, he read about the case as he ate his salad and headed upstairs to his room with a beautiful view and floor to ceiling windows. He sat next to the window and opened his laptop and looked up the base on Google earth it was scrubbed from the site, he opened a secure file on Jack Brown, he was working on the money trail, some of the agents were getting paid off, last had contact in Santa Monica, last text was Mona 3rd floor. He called Thomas he said, "Scramble 767, ok what do you know of this Jack Brown guy, was he one of yours?"

Thomas said, "No, he is not one of my agents, but I have heard he was one paranoid guy, he was hunting down Spectre it has infiltrated the workplace, you don't know who to trust, people are disappearing." Mark said, "Well that is nice to know, that dealing in Chicago felt like I was dealing with something bigger than the mob." Thomas said, "It's the same thing but worldwide organized crime, don't quote me on this, and I have nothing to back it up with, but I am thinking it is the old KGB."

Mark chuckled and said, "Something like politics, well I will see if I can find some clues up here, I think I will head to Smith Tower see if there are any agents lurking about." Thomas said, "We have gotten their demands, they want the World to pay five trillion dollars that is with a T," Mark said, "So you are stalling till we find them right?" Thomas said, "Next Saturday they take down three more satellites, and that will destroy a hundred with all the debris, nothing will be safe, we are talking phones, TV, GPS, weather, shit is going to get real." Mark said, "A week, well I had better be getting dressed then, I have to go my food is here."

He quickly ate, showered off the sunscreen he had on from Hawaii, and dressed in business casual. He headed down to the bar and got a bottle of coke for the ride. He had a cab waiting for him when he got in he said to the driver, "Smith Towers please. I believe it is in Pioneer Park." The driver said, "Ok I believe it is Pioneer Square, did you know at the time when it was built in 1914 it was the tallest skyscraper this side of New York, at 38 stories?" Mark said, "It has a real nice bar up on the 35th floor."

The driver dropped him right in front of the building. He put on his shades; they were Google glass and the facial recognition software put a name to almost every face and employment. He walked into the elevator and said to the operator as he slipped him a twenty, "Up to the bar my good man." The man smiled and said as the door closed, "We just redid the cable system and kept the old time look, and we slow to a nice stop." Mark said, "Very nice it must take a few tries to get it." The operator said, "I don't have the patience to train people, it is funny watching though, stop too fast and it will take you right off the floor."

Mark stepped off the elevator into a large open space window all around and a uniquely carved chair, he walked over to it, as he was taking in the place. He ran his hand over the craved dragon arms each held a ball in its mouth. A man walked up and said, "Don't sit in that, bad juju, they say if you sit in the chair, you will be married within the year." Mark said, "Whoa, that is bad juju, so 735 that's Alex right?" The man reached out his hand and asked, "666, what the hell are you doing here, you are supposed to be dead?"

Mark smiled and asked, "So what is the story of the chair?" Alex said, "Read the sign, it was given to the builder of the place L.C. Smith here it is by the Empress Dowager Cixi in 1908, shall we get a quick drink?" Mark said, "A quick one, you know why I am here." They walked into the bar. Mark scanned everyone, he would highlight their faces and a name would pop up with their occupation. Alex raised his hand as he got to a table in the corner, a waitress came over and he asked, "Can I get you a vodka martini with a shot of orange liqueur?" Mark said, "Not tonight I will have what he is having and put it on his bill." The waitress asked, "Is that alright sir?" Alex looked Mark in the eye and said, "That's fine." Mark asked, "Can you put one of those big smoked ice cubes in it?" Alex said, "This is 23 year old Pappy Van Winkle; you don't want to dilute it." Mark smiled and said, "I will have the ice please."

Alex asked, "Ok why the hell did they put you on this case?" Mark smiled and said, "I just don't think they know who to trust, have you been to the doctors work site?" Alex asked, "Are you wearing Google glass, that is so old school? I personally have not been to the base, we have people working on it." The waitress came over with his drink and sat it in front of him, it had a huge ice cube with an inch of bourbon surrounding it. Mark lifted the drink put it under his nose and inhaled, then swirled the big ice cube and took a sip, swished around his mouth ad swallowed, waited for a couple of seconds and did it again this time he closed his eyes cocked his head then said, "This is very nice, if you get over to the Four Seasons they have a very nice bottle of cognac Remy Martin have it with a drop of cherry juice."

Alex said, "You're not going to get in the way are you?" Mark smiled and watched an Oriental girl walk in his Google glass highlighted her face a name popped up Mary Summer, work visa from Xong enterprises, then a side bar came up, with another name Zhen Yang, MSS ten years, Foreign Intelligence. Mark lifted his glass and finished it, and asked, "So you are waiting for a report from the government what Doctor Adam Johnson was working on?" Alex said, "Should be coming any time now." Mark asked, "So you trust our government?" Alex said, "Well yes, and it is a secured base, it the middle of nowhere."

Mark stood and said, "Well I hope everything goes well, I have a week to crack this case, thanks for the drink." Alex stood and held out a card and said, "You find something tell us; we have to stop this it is top priority." Mark said, "Sure whatever, he took the card and put it in his wallet." Alex asked, "What if I want to contact you?" Mark smiled and shook his hand and said, "You won't." He turned and walked away, toward the observation room; he walked up to the girl and said, "We meet again, Mary Summers, I believe."

She turned and looked at him and said, "James, no wait Mark Neal, so what is the bad boy 666 doing in Washington again?" Mark said, "Why don't you have a seat in the chair?" Mary said, "Oh no you don't, you sit in it." Mark sat and looked up at her and asked, "Do you have a car?" She said, "Yes." Mark smiled and said, "I will meet you at the club in Colombian Towers in a half hour." She smiled and said, "Yes, a half hour, order champagne."

He walked to the elevator and went down to the lobby, he called an Uber and his ride was three minutes away, so he took in the beautiful marble, and the brass of all the elevators, played tourist, then straight out the door to his awaiting ride. He got into the Uber and said, "Colombian Towers please, and could you do a couple of laps around a block somewhere, I think my boss is having me followed," he held out a hundred dollar bill. The driver said, as he took the bill, "I will keep an eye out."

Mark said, "I know you think I am paranoid but this does happen." The driver said, "You know if you have a company phone they can track you on that." Mark said, "That is true, I have had my phone wiped professionally, and it is my phone, and it's not like the government trying to find me if so computers are really smart." The driver said, "Blue sedan, three cars back is copying every move we take, should I lose him?" Mark said, "No that is fine, just get into the outside lane and I will get out, I have a ride on its way." He got out of the car and waved at the guy in the blue sedan, the window lowered and he could see the man pulled his gun out and start to point it at him, Mark ducked and took a few quick steps to some cover, he said to himself, "I am out of shape for a foot race." He looked at his phone and got into a car and slouched in the back seat, and said, "Straight to the Columbian Tower please."

They arrived at the tower; Mark said, "This is a tall one." The driver said, "It is 76 stories; it is the tallest building in Seattle, and it is over 300 feet taller than the Space Needle. Mark stepped out and quickly got inside without looking up, he went to the desk and said, "Hi I am early, I am meeting Mary Summers she is a member of the club." The woman said, "Would you like to wait?" Mark said, "No I am supposed to order drinks and an appetizer, now the last time I was here, there were only a couple of elevators that went to the top."

The woman said, "There are 48 elevators, Dave will escort you up and get you a table." Mark said, "Ok Dave we want a table not in the sun." He smiled and said, "Brother you're in the right place; we don't see much of the sun here." Mark peeled off a twenty from his money clip and held it up for the operator, he said to Dave "It is nice to tip, it shows you appreciate the job someone is doing, and I have to ride down, nothing worse the a jam packed car, you know how many diseases humans carry." Dave smiled and said, "This is a quick elevator around seventy five seconds, if you get a bad driver they can take you right off your feet with the breaks, and that's not funny is it Tom?"

The operator smiled ear to ear, and said, as he slowed the elevator, "That was an accident, he damn near hit the ceiling, and it is almost like being in space for a second." Mark said, "So you have to know what you are doing." Dave said, "There is some skill to it, some people can do it, others can't, most of the elevators are automatic." Tom said, "It's a living, but it can be boring as hell, the observation deck is busier with all the tourists, and here we are."

Dave said, "Let me check and see what table is available, would you like a corner table, it looks like Mary Summers prefers that one, and would you like her regular champagne a local Gloria Ferrer 2005 it is just over a hundred dollars a bottle?" Mark asked, "Do you have a Dom Perignon 2004 Brute Rose." He smiled as he said, "Yes we do, it is just north of $800.00 a bottle." Mark said, "That will be fine, and a cheese plate with Beluga caviar, just put it on her bill." Dave said, "It is ordered, if you would like to step this way."

Mark walked a couple of paces behind him casing the joint, he lifted his arm and put two fingers to his forehead in a salute to a man, his glasses said, Boris Pickofski KGB, danger level high. The man did a double take like he had just seen a ghost. They got to the table, in the corner Mark could see why she liked it so much it had a beautiful view of the sound and you could see Mount Rainer. Mark held up a fifty and said, "Thank you Dave, you have a good day." A young girl came up with a couple of glasses and a pitcher of water.

As she set down the glasses and started to fill them, Mark said, "Miss would you bring that man in a gray suit five tables over, the one that keeps glancing over this way, a shot of cognac on a large ice cube if possible, and I noticed you have a bottle of rare cask Remy Louis Martin Xlll with no price, just four dollar signs, put it on this card please, and if you will hand the man this note?" The note said, "Not dead just retired." She smiled and said, "I will check on that sir." A man came over with a silver champagne holder, then the appetizers, and champagne. The girl served the man the cognac, he looked at the note then raised the glass in Mark's direction.

Mark waved him over, the man stood adjusted his suit it was a well-tailored Armani suit, you could tell he was well built; he stood tall as he walked over. Mark said, "Boris you old bastard, it has been a long time." He smiled and said, "The beast, I thought you were dead, hell I even gave a toast to your death, by the way this is nice," he raised his glass. Mark said, "It should be it is two hundred and fifty a shot, so what do you know of the satellite killer." Boris said, "They brought you back to the job for this, what the hell? You should have stayed dead." Mark said, "This is just a hobby, I am Mark Neal, Private Eye at your service, now what do you know?"

Boris scooped up some caviar and put it on a piece of dried sourdough bread and said, "Not much, just some doctor in a secret base was working on a laser, and he went missing like six days ago." Mark asked, "Well did you toss his office?" Boris said, as he took a bite, "It is a strong military base, more security than you need, something isn't right here, what do you know about this?" Mark said, "The CIA is waiting for the intelligence briefing that could be a couple of days, I just don't know what is going on with these new hires, there just isn't any drive." Boris said, "I know what you mean, the trail gets cold and we have a week, by the way I do like the caviar on the sourdough it is very nice." Mark said, "Here comes my meeting, keep in touch, good luck I am on your side on this."

Mary walked by Boris and said, with contempt, "Pickofski." He said, "Summers, what the hell are you doing here?" She held up a hand, and rolled her eyes as she walked by, straight to Mark's table she said, "What the hell is he doing here?" Mark stood, stepped over and pulled out a chair for he and said, "The same thing you are I would think, the satellite killer, if they blow up three satellites there will be so much debris a hundred will die, it could impact the Space Station." She said, "I see you have an old watch, the jammer is flashing, the new ones you can adjust the range."

Mark poured her a glass of champagne. She took a sip and purred, as she said, "This is so good, so tell me what have you learned." Mark said, "Well not much, this morning I was on a beautiful beach talking to some people about a re-tirement home, and I was rudely interrupted and brought here, so far I have learned damn near nothing. Doctor Adam Johnson has gone missing and he was some guy that worked on lasers. Have you been to his office to find any clues?" She put some caviar on a piece of cheese and asked, "Have you been to his office? It is well manned, more security then you need."

Mark said, "I haven't even been briefed about this, what do the Chinese have to say about this." Mary said, "Nobody knows who is behind this, once the money is paid, we can watch it and track down who takes it." Mark smiled and said, "I really don't think that is a good plan, they are showing power, this is an act of terror, they have the world shaking in their boots."

Mary asked, "You don't think it is about the money." Mark said, "Well yes it is always about money, but this is about power, who is behind it, why is there so much security at this army base, someone knows something and I think they are someone of power already." Mary said, "It has just happened, shall we give it a day or two and see what comes up?" Mark poured the last of the bottle and said, "We don't have a day or two, we must strike when the iron is hot, there is a u-boat out there with a laser on it, they could blast a major city, did you see that plasma charge?" She said, "A u-boat as in a World War two u-boat, there were just over a thousand built, and it can dive just under a thousand feet, you should be able to see it from the air. What type is it? There were a few models."

Mark said, "I haven't a clue, you don't have the video, why aren't we sharing this information? Give me your number, in fact here is my phone put your number in my contacts." She smiled and said, "A late night booty call, I could be up for that." Mark said, "I am too old to be playing these games, ok I will send you the video, and I am sure they updated the boat, but why a boat?" She said, "I would have put it in a plane." Mark said, "Too easy to track, a semi would have worked, there are thousands of them." She said, "That would be easy to track, there are cameras everywhere." He tapped his phone to hers and transferred the video, "Now make sure it is there," He scrapped the last of the caviar onto a cracker, as she opened the file. She said, "Not the best video, but it looks like a U-99 this is a museum piece."

Mark said, "Boy you know your world war two boats, and that's what I thought, there can't be many of those floating around, you would think it would be easy to find one that is missing." She said, "Ok I will share with you the video I have, it is from space." She loaded it and slid it across the table Mark lightly tapped it and you could see the laser hit a satellite then a ball of energy travel up that beam of light blowing it up, all in slow motion, he asked, "Can I have a copy of that."

She reached over and took the phone and said, "No of course not, that plasma is the power of a hundred sticks of dynamite, and that satellite was 1,800 miles above the Earth, now China has over 280 satellites circling the Earth, we don't want to see them destroyed." Mark said, "Wow that is really up there, is that the highest orbit, and the farther out the faster you would think it is flying." She smiled and asked, "Why didn't you stay dead? Oh and I think the highest is like 2,000 miles up, the lowest is like a 100, space starts at 62 miles." Mark said, as he stood, "Well I need a good night sleep; it has been a really long day, talk to your people, I will talk to mine and maybe we can get together on this, Miss Yang."

Her phone vibrated on the table, she picked it up and her face drained of color. Mark asked, "Is everything alright?" She held out her phone so he could see and said, "The aircraft carrier Shandong was hit by the laser, three thousand miles away, it blasted through the ship and hit the ammunition magazine, all five thousand crew were lost." Mark said, "It blew right through the steel hull, this is something, I am so sorry, I have your number I will keep you in the loop," he put his arm around her he looked at Boris, he looked up from his phone and shrugged his shoulders. Mark said, "I have to go; I will take care of this."

Mark headed to the elevators once inside he took out his phone and started to order a ride, the operator said, "Most phones will not work, it is only a minute ride." He closed his eyes when he opened them, they were at the lobby; he stepped out and ordered a ride back to the Four Seasons. Once he was there, he stepped over to the valet and told him, "I need my car sent over and I will be right down to get it, so don't park it far." He went to his room and dressed in black jeans, black tennis shoes, a loud Hawaiian shirt, and he grabbed a dark hooded sweatshirt and headed down to get his car.

He got to the valet as a dark blue Nissan Sentra pulled up. Mark stepped over to the car the man got out and texted him, his phone chirped. He said to the man, "I am Mark Neal," he gave him his valet ticket and peeled off a twenty-dollar bill and handed to him and said, "Thank you very much for the fast delivery of the car, I just have this last-minute thing up in Woodinville." Mark had the base already loaded on his phone, well a fish hatchery below it, because there was no base on the map. He got into the car and pulled out threading his way through the city the traffic was terrible, to his surprise the car handled very well, soon he was out in the countryside driving six miles over the speed limit.

He was heading for the fish hatchery, which was just north of the base, he pulled off the highway on a side street, and took out a small drone the size of a hummingbird, unfolded its propellers and slipped on a pair of glasses on, sat the drone on the roof of the car and it took off he was flying it with his phone and watching the video feed in his glasses. He went straight up then down the road a few miles, then hit home and the drone came right back to where it took off. Mark got back in the car and went down a couple of miles and pulled into a winery, and drove down a dirt path and parked in the vineyard.

He got out of the car and put on his sweatshirt and pulled up the hood, he headed into the thick woods, away from the road, he came upon a ten-foot electric fence, with a half dozen green buildings, he could see cameras every couple of hundred yards. He walked quietly towards a small creek where the fence hopped across it; he said to himself, "This sucks." He got to the creek and got down on his belly and did the belly crawl up to the fence and slipped under and got to his feet and moved quickly from tree to tree, then to a building he slipped around it and seen a guy pushing a garbage can on wheels, he followed him into the building started small talk, when the guy got to the janitors closet, he hit him with a stun gun. He quickly took the man's jacket and zip tied his hands and feet.

Then, he grabbed him by the jaw and squeezed as he asked, "Where is Dr. Adam Johnson's office?" The man said, "He is gone, we cleaned out the office." Mark squeezed tighter the man said, "Third floor in building 29." Mark asked, "Did he have a laboratory?" The man said, "Yeah in building 36." Mark said, "There are only a half dozen buildings here." The guy said, "I know I am not the one that numbered them, we have one it is building 112."

Mark took a roll of painter's tape and wrapped around his head like ten times taping his mouth shut, the put on the jacket and emptied out a mason jar that held steel scrubbing pads in and filled it with bleach, pushed a button on his watch and a small strip stuck out the side, he pulled out the strip and peeled off the back paper and stuck it to the glass, and sat it in a bucket, then poured a whole bottle of ammonia in the bucket, and headed out the door. He used the badge to open the next building and went to the third floor to the office of Adam Johnson, the place was spotless, nothing in the garbage cans, no computers, no pictures.

He said, "Damn." He picked up his bucket and headed for the next building, he stopped and looked at a map of the place, building 112 was the building he was just in. He turned around and went into that building, he took the stair well to the basement, to his surprise it was full of people, he sat down his bucket and took out a small cartridge from his pocket and put it in his mouth then pushed a button on his watch to pop the jar in the bucket and chlorine gas filled the hallway, he walked down the hall with people running all around heading for and exit. He looked in a few laboratories one had a picture of Dr. Johnson and his son.

He walked in and tried to boot up one of the computers, but he didn't have the pass code, he pulled out a USB and plugged it into the computer, he walked around and kept on looking at the blinking light on the USB, soon it blinked green. He pulled it from the computer and took off in a full run towards the door, he reached for his gun but he didn't have one, as soon as he opened the door the bright lights hit him. He said, "Shit" and he pulled off the jacket and was back in his dark sweatshirt, he slid into the shadows of the building. People were heading for the office building, and security were propping the doors open and airing out the building, alarms were ringing. Mark got to a point he ran from the building to a shadow of a tree and followed it to the creek, he slid down the bank of the creek slipping into the water, he stayed low and in the dark until he was under the fence.

Mark got out of the water he heard a hum than saw a red and green light in the sky, he said, quietly "Damn infrared," he looked at the field of grapes he parked the car, it was lighted like it was day, he slid back in the cold creek. He pulled out his phone and said, into it "I need an extraction, I am being hunted by drones," he pinged his phone. A voice said, "You have a couple of miles till you hit the Snoqualmie River stay in the creek you're giving off electromagnetic radiation, once you get to the fork in the river then ping you location again, turn off your phone till then."

Mark kept to the shadows as he floated down the creek, going under whenever a drone flew over, he came close a small bridge where a couple of army personal were standing talking. He reached for his gun, again he realized he didn't have one, he reached into his pocket and put the cartridge back into his mouth, and felt around on the bottom for a rock, he held it on his chest and floated under water for a couple of hundred yards past the bridge every so often there was a tree laying across the river to stop boats from motoring up to the base.

It was just breaking dawn when Mark reached the Snoqualmie River, he looked at lights in some of the houses, he pulled out his phone and pinged his location. He heard an engine pick up speed, and an airboat without anyone in it pulled up. He reached the side and pulled himself aboard a voice said, "Well 666 it has been a while." He said, with his teeth chattering, "My God I am frozen." The voice said, "Well we have company, three boats are coming from upriver," two wings slid out the sides of the airboat and it started to pick up speed. Mark wrapped his arms around himself trying to warm up the boats behind him were catching up as the airboat left the water and flew five feet above and left the pursuing boats behind. Mark yelled, "What the hell? We are above the falls."

The voice came on and Mark could only hear, "This should work." Mark pulled out his phone pressed it against his head so he could hear and yelled, "What?" A screen lit up and a man said, "This should be beautiful; I wish I was there." Mark got to his knees and said, "Where are you taking me." The man said, "Three miles down the river is a boat landing I have a trailer waiting for you there." Mark said, "That's on the other side of the falls."

The man said, "Don't worry, it all works out on paper, the falls are a 268-foot drop, this should work." Mark said, "I am freezing, do you have a gun in this thing?" The man said, "It is a prototype a guy in Chicago builds them, I just tweaked it a bit. Is it a smooth ride, do you hear the falls?" Mark peeked over the front of the boat to see the river disappear, he yelled "I am going to die," the boat flew off the edge of the falls quickly descending into a mist of the falls hitting the river hard slamming Mark to the floor of the boat, the boat lifted back off the water and flew down the river, it settled down onto the water and pulled right up a ramp into the back of a truck. Mark said, "Desmond I am going to kick your ass, where am I going?" The man came on the screen and said, "To your hotel, I figured you could use a nice warm shower after swimming all night, you might want to check for leeches."

Mark asked, "Could I ride up front." The truck pulled off the highway and the door opened and the ramp cane out. Mark walked down the ramp to a bright sunny morning, he stepped over to the truck and got it finding out there was no driver. He said, "That figures, you don't mind if I turn up the heat, do you?" A voice said, "Turning up the cabin heat to what temperature?" Mark said, "80-degrees Fahrenheit." He put on his seat belt and went to sleep.

Mark awoke with a voice saying "You have arrived at your destination, thank you and have a nice day." He got out of the truck, and the truck pulled away. He was still soaked to the bone, he got up to the governor's suite, to find a Miss Summers standing there in one of his shirts and nothing else. Mark said, "Well, Miss Yang imagine meeting you here." She said, "It's Mary Summers to you, and you didn't come home last night." Mark rolled his eyes looked at her and said, "It has been a long night, is there anything to eat?" She said, "You're a mess, and you are soaked."

Mark smiled and said, "Let's take a shower, you can check me for bloodsuckers." She chuckled as she said, "I bet you say that to all the girls, quite the come on." Mark started to peel off his shirt. She said, "You weren't kidding, there is one stuck right in the middle of your back." Mark said, "I haven't been that cold in a long time, I am getting way too old for this." Mary said, "You swam down the creek."

Mark said, "Down the creek to the river then over the falls, it has been a busy night," he sat on the toilet and took off his shoes and socks. Mary asked, "Was it worth it, did you learn anything?" He took off his pants and went thru the pockets, he held up his wallet and said, "There is nothing worse than getting your wallet wet." She said, "Come on slowly turn, there's one the back of your thigh." He said, "Well pick it off."

She said, "You can reach that one." Mark slid his hand down the back of his leg found it and grabbed onto it and pulled it off, then dropped it in the toilet, she checked him over and looked through his hair finding two more small ones. He slid her shirt halfway off her shoulders and kissed her on the neck she said, "No way in hell, you stink, get in the shower." He said, "Call room service, I need a good cup of tea, and breakfast." She said, "I am getting dressed, what did you find?" She picked up the USB and headed out the door, she called room service and put in her order, then took a lipstick from her purse slid a panel off and plugged in the USB and uploaded it to her phone.

She came back to the bathroom where Mark was shaving with a towel wrapped around his waist. He asked, "Was there anything important on the USB drive?" She smiled and said, "Nothing, just operations, the computer was wiped clean." Mark looked at her and said, "Well that was a waste." Mary slid her arm around his waist and kissed his nipple, she looked up and said, "You smell a lot better, and it was better you than me, you didn't find anything right." Mark kissed her forehead and said, "Not a damn thing, what do you know of Jack Brown."

She slid her hands into the towel and grabbed him by the butt cheeks and said, "Jack Brown, he disappeared like 12 days ago, he was working on the mob or something, nothing to do with me." Mark smiled "He was a little paranoid, always talking about that old Spectre mob, I am thinking he might be right, that was our, well my army trying to kill me." She smiled and said, "They didn't know who you were, and breakfast should be here soon." The door chimed Mark asked, "Woman's intuition." She said, "I see death in your future, unless you take it more safely, there was a reason nobody checked out the doctor's office it was heavily guarded."

She opened the door and two men came in one pushing a cart the other setting the table, Mark picked up his phone and booked a flight to Los Angeles, he asked, "How long to get to the airport." A waiter said, "Around twenty minutes depending on traffic." Mary smiled and asked, "Where are we going?" Mark started to take his wallet apart and set everything on a clean towel, he handed one of the waiters a wet twenty, and said, "Sorry about that, I was pushed into the pool last night." Mark said, "Sit let's have a quick breakfast, have I told you how beautiful you are this morning."

She smiled and said, "No you haven't, so where are you going." Mark said, "I am hunting clues, we have a week before they blow up more satellites, this time there will be so much space debris it could take out hundreds all depends on what orbit they hit, and thank you for the crepes these are delicious, that was a miserable night, and going over the falls I thought I broke my ribs." She stopped with a fork full of hash, and asked, "You went over Snoqualmie falls, and lived." He rolled his eyes up to meet hers and said, "I was in a boat, an engineer said, it worked on paper, I guess it did but not that well, I flew fifty or a hundred yards from the falls but dropped like a rock hitting the water hard." He got up with his tea and went into the bathroom and started to blow dry his money clip and everything that was from his wallet. Mary picked up a card and said, "You're a licensed private investigator, impressive, so you are a private dick."

He said, "Here why don't you do this while I get dressed, this case is getting cold as we speak." She said, loudly "You never said, why you didn't stay dead." Mark came back in dressed, with a shirt and a tie, he said, "They don't trust some of the younger agents, something is up, and this is a favor to my old boss." She looked up at him and ran her hand along his jaw line and asked, "Would you keep me in the loop? I will help as much as possible."

He pulled his phone from his pocket looked at it to unlock it and said, "Put your number in it, under Summers, this is something you didn't know, I am looking for a wife, well I am looking for a retirement place and it would be nice to share it with someone." She looked shocked, as she asked, "Are you asking me to marry you?" Mark said, "Well not really, maybe, I don't know, it just would be nice to share my life with someone, just think about it, or think of someone would fit the part."

She said, "Oh now I get it, you want me to hook you up with someone I am not good enough for you." Mark eyes popped wide open as he back peddled "I didn't mean anything like that, there are so many questions, are you ready to settle down? Will your government allow it, do you like me, do you want to have kids, where do you want to live, do you snore more then you used to? I mean I like you, and we do have a history, but what would it be like being with you 24/7?"

She stared at him and said, "Nope, not doing that, you're going to have to find someone else." Mark said, "See this is not that easy, you have to ask yourself are you ready to slow down and enjoy life, I am, but it just isn't happening I am working more now than ever, I have found out I am disposable, my last mission ever one on the team were dispensable, it was damn near a suicide mission." She said, "So how did that work out?" Mark said, as he leaned over to kiss her on the cheek, "We lost a few, keep me informed what is going on, and we can work together on this." She turned her head quickly and their lips met, she kissed him passionately and said, "There is plenty more where that came from, stay safe, you have my number."

Mark grabbed his luggage and Mary followed him down, he said, "Think about retiring, I might be a little old for you." She smiled and said, "I would watch your back on this one." Mark walked out to the valet and asked, for a taxi. The man hailed a taxi that was parked down the street. Mark walked to the back of the car and the driver put his luggage in the trunk, he said, "To the airport my good man, the Delta wing please." He got in and took a nap, the taxi driver pulled up to the Delta airlines, he tapped his brakes hard to shake Mark awake, he opened his eyes and the driver said, "We are here sir." Mark got out and the driver took his luggage from the trunk, he peeled off a hundred and handed it to the driver, and said, "Keep it." He walked up to the ticket counter and weighed his luggage, he ran his watch over the suitcase it blinked red, he just shook his head.

Chapter Three: To Los Angeles

He landed in LAX stood and waited for his luggage, saying to a guy, "One good thing about flying first class your luggage comes out first, and here comes mine." He grabbed his bags and headed out the door to find a taxi. He got in one and said, "Here is a hundred, I am your only fair to Santa Monica the Viceroy hotel." The man said, "Yes sir." They got on the 405 it was bumper to bumper, but they still made petty good time, the driver pulled up to the Viceroy hotel, he said, "Thirty-five bucks."

Mark peeled off two twenties and said, "Let me tell you it is better you driving in this crap than me." The driver smiled and said, "That wasn't bad at all, enjoy your stay." Mark took his luggage to the counter and showed the guy his phone and asked, "Could I upgrade to a better room with an Ocean view? I am not paying for this give me the best I can get." The man said, "Yes sir; let me see what we have, how many nights may I ask?" Mark said, "I would think just one I have to wrap up something and it had to be done in person."

The man said, "Ok we do have the Empire Suite it is 640 square feet, with a beach view, it is $371 per night." Mark said, "That will be fine," he got the key card and went up to his room, he put the suitcase on the bed opened it and scanned it with his watch, a light would blink red when he waved it slowly across it, he unzipped a compartment ran his hand through it and came up with a mini SD card, he ran the watch over the suitcase, it didn't blink when he ran it over the card it did. He smiled and walked into the bathroom and flushed the card.

He went to the bedroom and sat on the bed closed his eyes and said, "I have to keep moving," he looked in his suitcase it was still packed for the trip to

Hawaii he took out a Hawaiian shirt a pair of shorts and sandals, got dressed and stood in front of the glass wall looking over the beach. He went out to the paved walkway and hailed a pedicab to take him the short distance to the pier.

There were thousands of people on the pier, people fishing, drawing portraits, it is a big tourist location. He walked by the roller coaster and watched it for a second watching the people behind him, he made it to the restaurant on the end of the pier he stood there and looked at it, then walked in and checked the place out, turned and walked out. He walked around the place glancing at his watch. He walked over to the Pier Burger and got a burger and ate it on his way back off the pier, he stopped and watched a man catch a mackerel and put it in a pail. He walked past the Ferris wheel, he stepped up to a man with a broom and a dustpan and asked, "Is there any buildings around here that are three stories or higher?"

The man said, "All you have to do is go in town they are all three stories or higher." Mark walked up the street into Santa Monica; the man was right, there were quite a few high rises, there was shops and restaurants, he just wandered down the street, he walked into a mall, went up the escalators to the third floor and there was a huge picture of Marilyn Monroe; his watch blinked green he reached down and pushed the face of the watch until the green light went out. He turned and walked to the men section and shopped for a wallet. He got down to the street haled a pedicab with a twenty, he said, "To the Viceroy my good man." He got in and looked at his phone; it said, "Safe House, Chicago." He said, "Dammit all to hell," he booked a flight to Chicago. He got into the hotel and went right to his room, pulled out a Ziplock bag that held everything from his wallet and started to transfer everything back in, he called an Uber and went down to the desk and checked out.

Chapter Four: To Chicago

He got into the Uber and headed for the airport, soon he was in line getting his tickets, he had to fly with the cattle way in the back of the plane, and it was a five-hour flight. He had to sit in the middle of two people, the lady next to him pulled out a book. Mark asked, "What are you reading may I ask?" She smiled and said, "It is Deadly Treasure Hunt by Donald Richter." Mark said, "I did read some of his work, the book with the fairy war it was a trilogy, I still have to find the last book, on this flight I was hoping to get some rest; it was a long night last night."

She smiled and said, "This one is funny, he worked in a bunch of jokes into it, he just added a young boy so he could put little Johnny jokes into it, some of the jokes are pretty blue." Mark said, "That's nice; I have to get some sleep," he got to Chicago and did manage to sneak in a couple hours of sleep.

They landed and he got his luggage and went to a rental service and ordered a Ford Mustang he went to pick it up. The guy pulled up with the car and stepped out with a clipboard and under it was a stun gun he shot Mark and held the trigger down. Another man appeared and zip tied his hands and feet both of them grabbed onto him and tossed him into the trunk along with his luggage. They took him for a ride down to the docks; they stopped in front of a fishing boat. A large man walked to the trunk of the car the trunk was opened the man reached in and touched Mark with a hand-held stun gun, the big man put the stun gun in his pocket and reached in picked Mark up and throw him over his shoulder and stepped onto the boat.

A man said, "So Mister Neal, I hear we are going fishing, it is a nice night to fish." The large man laid Mark on a fiberglass board that was on wheels, he strapped him on it. A younger man came in with a five-gallon pail of crayfish, he said, "Now what we are going to do is to open you up and pour these crabs into your chest cavity and drop you to the bottom of the lake." A shot rang out, the big guy took a bullet to the head, then another shot the younger man took one to the chest. Another man stepped out of a van and took out the driver of the car. The van passenger's door opened and a man jumped out, three quick steps to the boat, the third man was starting the boat and a shot rang out he went down.

Two more men came out of the van and started to collect bodies. A woman pulled up she walked onto the boat and said, "Mister Mark Neal, this is your lucky day, Frank said you owe him one. Let's get you off this board and find out why someone wants you dead." She unstrapped him the men had the last of the bodies loaded. Mark said, "Let's hurry the cops will be here soon." She said, "This happens more than you would think, the high-powered rifle is a bit out of the ordinary, but it had a silencer." Mark said, "I have to call in a cleanup crew."

She smiled and said, "Already done, so how do you know Frank, he went out of his way to save your ass." Mark smiled and said, "I did a job in Chicago, not too long ago, they killed an accountant, I was hired to find the murderer, and it got complicated, I am getting too old for this." The woman said, "Do you want the car? I will have it driven to your hotel." Mark said, "How the hell do you know where my hotel is, I haven't even been there yet?" She smiled and said, "You're staying at the Congress; I was surprised at that."

Mark said, "I like the location and many presidents stayed there; it has history." She said, "Would you like to drive or shall I?" Mark said, "Hold on, wait a minute, you're coming with me." She smiled and said, "No you are coming with me; your luggage is sitting next to my car." His rental car pulled away, then she said, "Mister Neal I am Patty Bottom, and you are my responsibility now, how long are you staying in Chicago?" Mark said, "You can drive, I take it am not going to be returning the rental, now did you say your name was Patty Tom?"

She smiled and said, "The car will be taken care of, you will never get the blood smell out of it, it is easier just to scrap it, it is amazing how much blood you get from a head shot." Mark said, "This doesn't bother you?" Patty smiled as she popped the trunk and said, "I work in Chi-town, this is just another day."

They got into the car she said, "No it is Bottom, you know those guys in the office, I was Penny Wise for the first three years of service, and so what are you doing in town?" Mark looked at her and asked, "Bottom that is English right?" He wondered if he could trust her, then said, "I am chasing a clue, which is Safe House, do you know where it is?" Patty chuckled and said, "There are dozens of safe houses in this city, the one you are probably thinking is a restaurant, and it's a dance place at night." Mark asked, "Have you been there?" She smiled and said, "Many times, but you have to remember someone wants you dead, if you would like to go you could stay with me, I am like 5 blocks from the place."

Mark smiled and said, "I have a hotel booked, and as you said, someone wants me dead." She smiled and asked, "Are you sure you don't want to come to my place?" He smiled and said, "No that is fine, so is this a black-tie place?" She smiled and winked then ran her tongue across her lips then softly said, "No you can leave your tux, just put on something nice, ok we are here." Mark asked, "I thought you were coming to the club with me?" She popped the trunk and said to the Valet, "He is checking in." She looked over to Mark and said, "I will give you an hour, could I have your number? I will give you a call when I get here." Mark handed her a card, it was Mark Neal, Private Eye, with his phone and e-mail.

Mark got out and walked around handed the valet a ten and took his luggage. He went in showed the girl his phone and got his room to his surprise it was the same room he had the last time he was there, a nice view of Buckingham fountain overlooking Lake Michigan, he could see the Ferris wheel on the Navy pier, the other way was the Sheds Aquarium, behind that was the Planetarium. He took out his phone and went into the cloud to retrieve Frank's number, then called it. Frank answered and said, "Mark it is good to hear you are still alive, the lake can be a bit cold this time of year." Mark said, "Hey I really owe you one, how did you know?"

Frank said, "You don't owe me anything, you're family, I keep my ears open, there are more players in the game for some reason they are getting a little braver, but I would watch your ass." Mark smiled and asked, "You know where the Safe House is?" Frank said, "Yeah it's over by Trader Joes, just a few miles from here, where are you staying?" Mark said, "Over at the Congress, is that the only safe house around?" Frank said, "Oh you're looking for a safe house, well there are a ton of them in town, did you think of the Rainbow house? There are safe houses for runaways, hookers, the cops have a few, what are you looking for?" Mark said, "I have no idea, this is just something I am following up on, what is the dress for this place?"

Frank chuckled and said, "It is a theme restaurant the steaks aren't bad, the burgers are very good it is a family place before eight, I take the wife and kids they get a kick out of it. I will send a couple of boys out there and make sure you don't go swimming." Mark asked, "You know of a broad called Patty Bottom?" Frank said, "We have had some dealing with Miss Patty. She is CIA, her last name is Bottom that's funny, is that who they sent? I would have thought they would have sent you a veteran, not saying she isn't talented, and she does have a nice ass but sometimes you need muscle." Mark said, "Well thank you again, so how is the partnership going?" Frank said, "Everything is going better than I expected; the project in Vegas is taking off, and Tony and I are running a tight ship."

Mark said, "Ok I am going to ask straight out; do you know of anything about the satellite killer?" Frank said, "Oh my God, you're on that case, it was on the news, did you see that laser shooting in the sky? I think it is the Chinese, they have done it before." Mark said, "I really don't think it is the Chinese, Christ they just lost an aircraft carrier and five thousand men, I know they have proven they can do it, but they have just as much to lose as the rest of the world." Frank said, "Really they lost an aircraft carrier, well I can't help you there, I wish you well this could really throw a wrench in the communications." Mark said, "It was a laser shot over three thousand miles away, blasted right through the steel hull into the magazine, everyone died, well I think, I just watched the video."

Mark opened his suitcase, it had short sleeved shirts and shorts, it was still packed for Hawaii, he opened his garment bag and took out his tux, then a suit coat inside that was a black shirt and dress pants. He took a quick shower and the desk called him saying Patty was downstairs, he had her come up. When she got there, he was just finishing getting dressed, he left her in and studied her she was Blonde, five foot five, around a hundred and thirty-five pounds wearing a short red dress with a light blue top button down to show her cleavage, he asked, "So what have you learned? I am not in the loop, I don't get the status reports, we only have a week to crack this."

She walked in and looked out the window and said, "I have forgotten what a beautiful view you have here, and no I am not on that case I am babysitting you." Mark said, as he wrapped his arms around her, and laid his chin on her head, "There could be worse jobs." She turned and said, "You almost died today; you could be at the bottom of the lake." Mark said, "About that, why so old school, who drops you in the lake anymore?"

Patty said, "Doesn't that bother you." Mark said, "Yes I am supposed to be retired, so do you work for Thomas." She said, "He retired years ago, where have you been." Mark looked her right in the eyes and said, "Shall we go down to this safe house and see what happens? I could use a bite to eat." Patty said, "You look tired, and I could use a drink." Mark smiled and asked, "Do you have a gun? You're going to have to protect me, I am unarmed, and all this flying is killing me." Patty asked, "So where were you coming from? It looked like you were in the Caribbean."

Mark said, "Let's go, I was looking at some property in Hawaii, I need a retirement home, and for some reason people in Hawaii are happy." She slid her arm around him and said, "Come on old man let's get going, I have a couple of agents there, everything will be fine." Mark asked, "Should I call an Uber?" Patty said, "Let me take care of this, it's only a two-mile ride." Mark said, "Way too far to walk," he pulled out his sunglasses, with a touch of his phone the glasses turned clear, he looked at her and asked, "How long have you been on the job?" She smiled and said, "Eight years, four in the field." He said, "Damn, they aren't updating my software, how am I supposed to work without tools?" She asked, "Is that Google Glass? Oh my God I read about these, they are so outdated."

They went out and a car pulled in, she said, "This is our ride." They got in and Mark said, "Good day Andre, he is 43 years old, has been with the service for twenty years, graduated from Kent state, and has a low security clearance." She reached over and took his glasses and put them on, then said, "These are cool, and I didn't think he was that old." Mark asked, "Do you have a wife and kids?" He smiled and said, "I have a husband, we are too old for kids, and we are never home."

Patty said, "No way, you're, gay that makes sense, boy you learn something every day." Mark asked, "You do know where we are going?" Andre said, "To the Safe House, so how long are you going to be there?" Patty said, "I suppose till they close." Mark said, "Oh hell no, a couple of hours, how much time should we give you?" Andre said, "I will be within ten minutes."

They pulled up in front of the place there was no sign just a red door, Patty said, "Well this is it." Mark asked, "Are you sure? There is no sign." She said, "If you were paying attention, there are small signs saying espionage and an arrow, you just have to follow them." Mark asked, "Really?" She said, "Don't worry this is the Safehouse." Mark asked, "Do you trust your fellow agents? I have some muscle here watching my back also."

She asked, "Do you think there is a mole?" Mark said, "What I think is anyone can be bought, if you paid Andre enough, he could have shot us right in the back seat, this is a dog-eat-dog business." Patty said, "You paint a poor picture of people." They walked in the door, Patty stepped up to a man sitting behind a desk and whispered in his ear, he pushed a button and a door opened. Mark walked up the man asked, "What is the password?" He looked at him and said, "What the hell? You left her in." The man asked, "Do you know the password?" Mark pulled out his money clip and peeled off a fifty and said, as he handed it to him, "Grant." The man took the bill and said, "Good enough for me."

Mark walked into the place it was huge; he stepped up to Patty and smiled. She said, "You are such a fun sucker," she turned to the girl behind the podium and said, "My party is here." They followed her to a table; a man walked by and gave Patty a slap on the ass. Mark said, "737 long time." The man stared at Mark for a second and said, "James, the Beast" Mark held out his hand and said, as he shook his hand, "It is Mark Neal, I am a private investigator, I gave up the job."

The man said, "Sam Smith, I don't get out in the field much, Patty this is 666 the beast that must mean your number is up for grabs, he killed an agent for it." Mark said, "If you would look at my record, I am dead, they just keep pulling me back into service." Sam said, "I don't know what the hell you got yourself into, but there are some heavy here tonight, and they are carrying some fire power." Mark smiled and said, "They are my keepers, a friend said he was sending some muscle." Sam said, "Well let me tell you that is some muscle, I called in a couple more agents." Mark asked, "So what is up with the laser satellite thing?" Sam said, "I don't know anything about it, the whole world seen it on the news, is that what you are working on?" Mark said, "Yeah the trail is getting old, I think I miss read a clue."

They took a seat and Patty said, "Your 666 the beast, I studied some of your cases." Mark said, as he looked at the menu, "I need a coke, and I will have the provocateur, with C-4 cheese curds." Patty said, "I will have the Mata Hari's meatloaf; would you like to order right away." Mark said, "I am starving, I am getting too old for all of this running around, and I am going to the men's room." He got up and kept looking at his watch, he walked all the way around the place looking at everything, and he looked like a tourist. He got back to the table and Patty asked, "Did you find what you were looking for?"

Mark said, "This is a neat place, it would be fun for the kids, but I found nothing, I have a bad feeling about this, and is there a lot of heat here damn near everyone is carrying." Patty said, "I see at least five agents, and a few mobsters, I saw you talking to the boss Tony; he is the Don." Mark smiled and said, "Nobody has heard of our dear Doctor Johnson, and Tony is well connected, he is looking to lose big time if the satellites are taken out, has anyone looked at who has been buying fiber optic stock?" Patty said, "This is not my field, I am here to keep you alive, and that would be just common sense to look into the competition."

Mark took a bite of his burger and said, "This is really good, and they must marinate the cheese curds." Pat said, "The food is good here, a little pricey if you were going to take the family, so how do you know Tony?" Mark took a long pull off of his drink and asked, "So what is this?" Patty said, "I ordered you your coke and an adult drink, it is a Spy Jolt iced coffee, vodka, and Kahlua, and something else." He picked it up and took a sip, then a bigger drink, and nodded as he started to finish his burger. Patty reached over and took his fork and speared some of her meatloaf and handed it to him. Mark took a long pull off his coke and finished it, took the fork and tried it and said, "This is really good." Patty said, "It is, isn't it? Less carbs, and here comes our desert."

A waitress said, "Agents, your Fat Bastard, with two spoons." Mark stared at the sparkler burning on the top of the ice cream, brownies, chocolate cake, whipped cream and chocolate sauce, he said, "Really, I am fat enough as it is." She smiled and said, "Put out the sparkler first." Mark took the sparkler and dipped it into his water.

After the meal Mark took her out on the dance floor and danced a couple of songs. Every once in a while an agent would dance by and grab her by the ass. She wrapped her arms around his waist and kissed his neck and said, "I can't wait for a name change." He lifted her off the floor and said, "Let's get out of here." She smiled and said, "Back to my place." He smiled and said, "I really could use a good night sleep." She smiled and said, seductively "I don't snore."

Mark said, as they got into the car, "You go home, I will go to the hotel, and I will call you tomorrow." She said, "A walk by the Buckingham fountain would be nice." Mark said, "And very romantic; that would be really nice, but remember people are looking for me, driver drop me off first at the Congress Plaza." Patty looked at him and asked, "Are you sure?" Mark said, "You do know I am looking for a wife, maybe we can get together after this." She said, "You do know you are old enough to be my father?"

Mark smiled and leaned in and kissed her on the lips lightly and said, "But it would be fun." She said, "You are cute, but could you afford me?" Mark winked and said, "Oh yes, anything you would need I could get you." Patty smiled and said, "Where I come from that could be a new dishwasher, do me a favor and stay alive." The driver asked, "Was the mission a success?" Patty said, "I don't think so." Mark said, "I am grasping at straws, it was a shitty clue, Safe House Chicago, they are telling me there are dozens of Safe Houses here." The driver said, "This is the most popular one."

Chapter Five: To San Francisco

Mark went straight to his room and booked a flight to San Francisco, he said to himself "That was a waste of time." He was down at the street waiting for his ride to the airport, an hour later he was back in the airport, this time he got a first class ticket. It was six in the morning and this time he went to the Sir Frances Drake. He talked to the Beefeater who stood out front, and said, "I need a company car please."

A bellhop took his luggage and followed him into the hotel the woman looked at his phone and said, "We have a suite up on the 19th floor would that do?" Mark said, "That will be just fine, is it overlooking Union Square?" he peeled off a twenty from his money clip and gave it to the Bellhop. She said, "Yes, it is, and how long are you staying?" Mark looked at her and said, "At least for the night, I am sick of sleeping on planes."

He went down to the lobby and got a glass of lemon water, looked at the bar, the beautiful chandlers, he stepped into Scala's Bistro. He asked a waiter, "Could I get a cup of coffee and a donut really quickly?" He held up a twenty between his fingers. The man said, "Right this way sir, we have one of the best pastry chefs in the world, so you are in a hurry I would suggest the Éclair; the whipped custard is to die for."

Mark said, "A scone will be fine; I think the last time I was here they had a cherry one, and could you cool the coffee down so I could drink it?" The waiter sat him and was back in two minutes with the scone and a girl sat a coffee in front of him. Mark rolled his eyes to meet hers and said, "A bill please, and this scone is very good."

In five minutes, he was back outside talking to the Beefeater, waiting for his car. The Beefeater said, "Your Glock slimline, five clips and holster are in the glove compartment, and 666 bring back the car without a scratch please." Mark smiled as a spotless Lincoln pulled up, he smiled and said, "This is just a fact-finding mission, I will have it back in a couple of hours." He got in and slowly pulled out into the street running on his phone's GPS. He had Doctor Johnson's address programmed into it already; it was in the Mission district not far from where he was."

He got onto Van Ness Avenue and was there in a few minutes, there was no parking anywhere, he pulled into the driveway and parked, behind a car leaving him parked blocking the sidewalk. He walked up to the house and knocked a man in a suit answered. Mark said, "Good day, I am Mark Neal private investigator, I have been hired by the family to find one Adam, the family is worried the police are dragging their feet." The man said, "That is nice what do you want?" Mark said, "Just to look around the residence."

The man said, "Wait here." Mark just pushed his way into the house and said, "No I think I will wait inside if you don't mind." The man pulled out his phone and made a call. Mark started to wander through the house with the guy following him, he walked through the master bedroom and down the hall to another bedroom, he was just scanning the room a picture frame with a green Mustang in it looked out of place, he picked it up, turned away from the guy, and sure enough, there was a picture of a Vegas show girl and a young boy behind it, it was signed, "To my little brother Lance." Mark folded it and put it in his pocket.

The man said, "Hey what the hell are you doing?" Mark said, "Do you feel something happened in this room?" The man said, "You might as well get the hell out of here; my boss said you need a search warrant, and he wanted me to check your paperwork, something that says you are a private eye and that you were hired by the Johnsons." Mark said, "You know there is something wrong here, if this is the kid's room, where is his laptop?"

The man got a call. Mark heard it, someone on the other end said, "That is 666 stop him." Mark said, "Time for me to leave." The man reached out and grabbed him, Mark took his hand twisted it and hit him with his palm in the shoulder popping it out of socket the man howled in pain as his arm dropped, he reached up with his other arm to hold it. Mark moved quickly to the door and jogged to the car. He seen another car pull out and followed him. He stepped on it, grabbing the emergency brake and turning sliding the car sideways, and then slamming the gas pedal to the floor.

When his car was sideways his window took a bullet from the car behind him, and it spider webbed the window. Mark said, "For Christ sakes," and then he flew down the side streets taking air off some of the cross streets. The car behind him matched him and was gaining on him, Mark suddenly slowed as the passenger held out a pistol and fired on him, hitting the back window, but the bullet proof glass held. Mark fired the laser out of the back of the car slicing open the radiator and whatever, steam flowed out of the hood and the car coasted to the curb. Mark turned downhill toward the Warf, he said to himself, "Crap; I have been made."

He wanted to get to the Fisherman's Warf area to blend in with the traffic, when out of the corner of his eye he saw a car picking up speed to match him at an intersection. Mark slammed on the brakes at the last second, the car flew through the stop sign Mark started to weave down the hill, soon he was on the Embarcadero and blended in with the traffic his phone took him to Market street then to Powell, he had to stop and watch the cable car come down the hill, he said to himself, "Now see if I was married we would ride the cable cars, walk down Fisherman's Warf, and just enjoying the day."

He drove up Powell to the Drake. He pulled up and said, to the Beefeater, "Sorry, you said, not a scratch, nothing about bullet holes, I need a new hotel better yet I will get my own." The guy looked at the car it had been shot a dozen times, a valet hopped in and drove it away." He walked in the hotel and went to the bar and asked, "Do they still make the Drake Manhattan, with their own Bourbon and maple syrup?" The bartender said, "Well yes we do; would you like one?" Mark pulled out a fifty and laid it on the bar and said, "Quickly please."

He walked to the restaurant and ordered a cherry scone, and asked, if it could be delivered to the bar. He turned around and got his drink and went up a beautiful marble staircase and sat next to the window, he looked at the picture he had taken from the Doctors house, he took a picture of it with his phone, the facial recognition did not work these people were scrubbed from the system. His scone arrived; it had a couple of strawberries with a slice of orange on the plate just to make it look nice. He typed into his phone as he quickly ate.

The search popped up it said, Atrium show room Luxor Las Vegas. He put his drink to his mouth tipped his head back and finished it in one swallow, and quickly went down the stairs to the elevator, and went straight to his room.. He pulled the garbage bag from the can and put his pistol holster and extra clips in it, he was back down at the street in five minutes. He checked out saying, "My boss doesn't know what he wants; I usually sleep on planes nowadays." He texted an Uber driver and walked out and handed the Beefeater the bag and said,

"It wasn't even fired." His ride showed up at the same time he looked at the driver's picture and license plate number and walked up with his luggage. The driver loaded it and off they went to the airport."

Chapter Six: To the Luxor

Mark flew into the McCarran airport in Vegas. It was a mad house, people all over the place everyone was excited to get their luggage and start their vacation. Mark stepped outside and got into a van, everyone told the driver what hotel they were staying at, on the way to the strip they stopped at the "Welcome to Vegas" sign, he helped take pictures. A woman asked, him "What are you excited to do here?" Mark smiled and said, "Sleep, this is a work trip."

She asked, "You want to come out for some drinks later?" Mark said, "I would love to, but that is not in the cards, I don't expect to stay the night if everything goes right." The van went to the back of all the casinos at one stop Mark slid him a fifty and said, "Front door please." The driver came around the block and pulled up under the huge Sphinx. One guy said, "That is two stories higher than the one in Giza, it stands 110 feet." Mark said, "That's interesting," he got off the van and took his luggage inside, walked through the doors took a right and there was the check in desk he walked up and said, "I need a room, anything will do, as long as it has a bed."

He took the key and headed to the elevators; he stopped and stared at it for a minute. A guy said, "They call them inclinators, they go up at a 39 degree angle, and no big deal until you have a few then you can feel it when you first move." Mark got in and sure enough he felt it go sideways, he went right to his room, sat his suitcase on the luggage rack, and hung up the garment bag. He was in his room for maybe five minutes; he went down to talk to the Concierge, then to the ticket booth to get a ticket to Rose's next show.

A man behind him said, "You had better ask where it is, I had to look for the Imax Theater and that has a seven-story screen, tonight we are going to the Blue Man Group." Mark rolled his eyes up to the girl selling the tickets and asked, "Do I really need directions to the Atrium?" She smiled and said, "Not really, go up to the mezzanine level, all the way back to the left, it is quite the walk, but it is the best Burlesque show in Vegas." Mark looked at his watch; he had an hour and 45 minutes before the show, he wondered around looking at the statues they were just huge. He went to the Hyper X Esports Arena, he looked at all the video games. A man said, "This place is huge it has 30,000 square feet of gaming; their tournaments bring people from all around the globe."

Mark headed to the Atrium where a comedy act was just leaving out, he walked up to a security man and shook his hand, slipping him a hundred and said, "I would like to see Rose Johnson, tell her I have news about her brother Marty." The guy looked in his palm of his hand and saw it was a Benjamin, he pushed a button and spoke into a microphone on his shirt, then he said, "There is a girl next to the corridor on you right she will take you to her dressing room."

Mark walked and found the girl he shook her hand palming her a twenty, and said, "Thank you very much, this should only take a minute." They walked a quarter of a mile to the dressing rooms, Mark said, "Where the hell are we going?" She smiled and said, "We are here; she does know you are coming right?" Mark said, "Yes I think so." The gal knocked on the door and a beautiful blonde girl answered, she was wearing short shorts and a crop top. Mark said, "Miss Johnson I presume, I am Mark Neal, Private Eye, I am looking for your father." She smiled and said, "Come in, Mister Neal what do you want with my father?"

He looked at his escort and asked, "Do you mind us doing this alone?" Rose said, "It's ok." The girl left and Mark walked into the dressing room and said, "That's a hell of a walk to get back here." She smiled and said, "We come in the back way it's only a few feet, so what do you want with my father?" Mark asked, "Did you see the news with the laser shooting down the satellite?" Rose said, "Do you think my father is behind that?"

Mark said, "Well some do, I think someone is using him and holding your brother as insurance. I would like to know where would your brother would hide, or do you know some where he would hole up." She asked, "Did you check the cabin?" Mark said, "What cabin? There is nothing about him owning a cabin." She said, "It is on the way to Muir Woods, up on a hill, did you ask Alex?" Mark said, "Ok who the hell is Alex?"

Rose said, "Let's try this, he is a real brainiac, Alexa video chat Alex." A voice said, "Video chatting Alex." A picture came up on the flat screen hanging on the wall. A young man sitting in his pajamas in a room full of monitors and keyboards, said, "Rose what is going on?" She asked, "Are you grounded again?" He smiled and said, "Six months, and who do you have with you?" Mark said, "I am looking for your friend Lance." Alex said, "What does the CIA want with Lance?" Rose looked at Mark and said, "CIA you lied to me."

Mark said, "I am retired; I was scrubbed from the system." Alex said, "You were scrubbed from a system, not the system, if you want to really disappear it is going to cost you." Mark asked, in a ruff voice "Do you know where the kid is or not?" Alex said, "I can turn on his phone and tell you were that is." Mark said, "Oh no don't do that, only if it is a last resort, if he is being held hostage that would tell them we know, do you know where the cabin is?" Alex said, "They are there, see the welcome sign is out in the front, that means someone is there, and there looks to be a large SUV parked in the driveway," Alex turned his phone so Mark could see a screen. Mark asked, "Do you have an address?"

Alex said, "You're 666 the beast, oh the address, here it is 4475 Ridge Ave, not Ridge road, it is the place up on the hill." Mark said, "Ok, back on the plane again, thank you for all your help." Alex said, "Do me a favor, text 75382 and send." Rose said, "Do it, he can help, he is a computer whiz, love you, Alexander." He said, "Yeah I wish, love you too."

Rose said, "My brother and Alex are always getting in trouble." Mark said, "Whoa, what is going on?" Alex said, "I am in there is nothing you can do; just relax you have some major firewalls." Mark said, "This is a company phone it can't be hacked." Alex said, "Everything can be hacked, don't worry, I will keep an eye on the cabin if anything happens, I will give you a shout out, now go."

Mark asked, "What is the quickest way out of this maze?" Rose said, "You are going to find my brother aren't you?" Mark said, "Well I think he is the key; I am having problems finding clues to this mystery, but I will try." She said, "Take a right, then the second hall take a left, there will be an elevator right there." Mark winked and headed down the hall, he got fifty yards then heard footsteps coming fast behind him, he looked back and started to run, he took two bullets to the back, a fire door shut between him and the shooter.

His phone asked, from his pocket, "Are you alright? My God you were shot." Mark groaned and said, "Oh my God, did that hurt?" He heard people running toward him, they grabbed him. Mark cried out in pain, then a "Who the hell are you?" A man picked a flattened bullet from his shirt, and said, "Really, this shirt is bullet proof." Mark said, "What the hell is happening?"

The other man said, to his microphone, "Yeah this is weird, we need a wheel-chair." The other guy said, "Check out the shirt, it is bullet proof, I bet it left a huge bruise." The man felt the shirt and said, "There is no way this could stop a bullet." Mark said, "It is made from spider web, they gene-splice a spider with a goat and extract the web from the milk." One guy asked, "You have to be kidding right? Well, we are going for a walk to see the Don."

Mark said, "I have places to be." One guy said, "We will see about that; the Boss doesn't like gun play in the house." They loaded him in the wheelchair and took him up to the Don's, one man asked, "Are we supposed to frisk him?" The guy asked, Mark, "Are you carrying?" Mark said, "No, I wish I was." They walked into an office a girl was sitting at the desk, she said, "He is waiting for you." They pushed Mark into a huge suite, Italian marble, chandlers, just beautiful, huge velvet curtains draped along two walls.

A man walked into the room and sat behind a black Granite desk, it had Luxor in gold inlay and fine gold lines, he said, "Agent 666 it is nice to meet you, I have heard you need a favor." Mark looked up and questioned "I do." The man said, "Yes you do, you are looking for a friend Lance Johnson, friend of Alex Edwin, now I do not like people getting shot in my casino and have heard you have endangered one of my girls." Mark said, "I guess I do need a favor, I need to get my stuff and get to the airport, so I can find your friend, and by the way who were those guys?"

The man came around the desk and held out his hand and shook Mark's saying, "I am Tony Breaker, I run this joint, don't worry about those two guy that shot you, they have been taken care of, nobody shoots my guests." Mark said, "I could call in some guys and have them questioned." Tony said, "They are on their way, everything will be cleaned up, now what can I do for you?" Mark said, "Well I need to get my stuff from my room and get to the airport; you wouldn't have some pain killers would you?" Tony pushed a button and the girl who was at the outside desk came out of the back.

Tony said, "This is not my office; this is my home. Sheila would you get Mister Neal a painkiller and a couple of Ibuprofen?" Tony asked Mark, "Did you break anything, and by the way I saw the shooting, where did you get a dress shirt that is bullet proof?" Mark said, "It is made of spider web and cotton." Tony said, "I got that bit, and a few companies are extracting web from goats, which I think is just wrong."

Sheila handed Mark a drink and a three Ibuprofen. He asked, after take the pills and washing them down with a refreshing Pina Colada. Mark said that Pina Colada was nice thank you. She said, "Actually it is a pain killer, and it is a double." Mark said, "Pretty much the same thing, thank you again." Tony asked,

"Can you walk?" Mark locked the wheels of the wheelchair and stood wincing of the pain, he said, "Holy shit, ok I can walk, alright I am good to go."

Tony said, "Sweetheart would you have Mister Neal's luggage brought down, and have a car take him to the airport?" Mark asked, "Do you have a private jet I could borrow?" Tony smiled and said, "I like you, but I do not want to be associated with you, understand." Mark said, "I understand it could be bad for business." Tony said, "No it could be unhealthy; you are playing with the big boys."

Sheila asked, "Did you book your flight so I know where to have you dropped?" Mark said, "We will make better time if I ride in the wheelchair," he stepped back to the chair and gingerly sat down. She said, to her watch, "I will meet you at the elevator, three minutes." Mark had his phone out booking a flight to San Francisco; he asked, "How fast can we get to the airport? I booked a flight that leaves in an hour."

She said, "Ten minutes, and another ten minutes to get to the Valet, your bags are there already." A young guy met her at the elevator and asked, "Is this the package?" Shelia said, "He has to make a plane so be quick about it." They stepped into the elevator; the guy pushed lobby. Mark said, as he held up a hundred, "My flight is in an hour, and I have to check my bags and go through security." The man said, "You're not going to make it." Mark smiled and said, "Have faith, do I have a car waiting with a driver?" The man said, "That I do not know, they told me your luggage is there."

The elevator door opened and the two of them were out at a sprint through the gaming floor, down the hall, to sliding glass doors, out to the valet, the man yelled "Joe I have that package, it needs to be on a plane in 45 minutes." The man raised his hand and a cab pulled up, they loaded his luggage and he got out of the chair slowly and tried to straighten up. The man took him by the arm and helped him to the car, once inside he said, "To the airport my good man, a hundred bucks if you hurry, I have a plane to catch."

They got to the airport; the driver asked, "Are you going to make it?" Mark gritted his teeth and said, "Just get my luggage, I will be fine," he had to lift his legs out of the car. The driver offered a hand and helped him out of the car. Mark handed him the hundred and said, "Thanks arthritis, it's hell to get old." To his surprise the airport wasn't jammed with people and he made his plane with three minutes to spare.

Chapter Seven: Finding Lance

Mark landed back in San Francisco, he got his luggage, and he could hardly stand straight because his back hurt that badly. He got out to the street and looked at his phone and pointed to a car then to the street in front of him. The car pulled up, the driver got out and said, "Mister Neal." Mark said, "Load my luggage, and to the Sir Francis Drake, I hate sleeping on planes." The driver asked, "First time in Frisco?"

Mark said, "No, this is a business trip; I have no time to play tourist." They pulled up to the Drake, Mark walked over to the Beefeater and said, "I need a company car." The man said, "No way in hell, the last one is still in the shop." Mark tried to stand straight and said, "Whatever I just need a car, and that package I gave you." The man said, "What happened to you?" Mark had a tear running down his face; he said, "It's hell to get old." He walked into the hotel carrying his briefcase and towing his suitcase with the garment bag riding on top, he went right up to the desk and ordered a room.

The girl said, "You had a room last night, didn't you?" Mark smiled and said, "Well that didn't work, we are going to try plan B. I want two queen beds overlooking the Union Square, this time I am going to spend the night, could I have the bellhop take up my luggage? I have to get to work." He walked over to the bar and held up a twenty catching the bartender's eye, and said loudly, "Two shots of Jameson neat." The bartender sat a glass in front of him and said, "What happened to you last night?"

Mark handed him the twenty and said, "I am getting too old to fall, keep the change," he put the glass to his lips and took both shots in one mouthful and swished it around in his mouth then swallowed. He sat the glass back down and said, "Well back to work." He walked back out to the street it was a sunny day, a trolley car full of tourist went by, and he walked up to the Beefeater and asked, "You got my car." He said, "This is just a rental, it is not a company car do you understand? No scratches, no bullet holes." Mark said, "I am just going for a ride in the country, did you put the package in the glove compartment?" The Beefeater smiled and said, "Just bring back the car in the same shape it is in, and yes your package is in the car." Mark chuckled, then grimaced showing he was in pain. The Beefeater said, "Maybe you should take a few days off." Mark said, "What do you mean? I am retired."

Mark looked at his phone then got into the car, it was a Ford fusion. The GPS on his phone took him right to a Walgreens. He found a spot to park and walked a half block back to the store. He bought a bottle of ibuprofen and a coke. He got back to the car and started out the GPS said, it would take 47 minutes, he drove over the Golden Gate bridge, the farther out of the city the less traffic. As soon as he was off the highway, the GPS told him to turn. Mark looked at the street sign and it said Ridge Road. He said, "Ah crap." He stopped and plugged in Ridge Ave. The GPS had him turn around, and in a few miles it said, "You have reached your destination."

Mark looked up the driveway, his phone said, "The SUV is still there, walk up the driveway stay to the right, they can't see you, walk straight to the corner of the garage, wait a second, there is a dirt bike on the other side of the house that shouldn't be there." Mark said, "Great, do you have real time photos?" Alex said, "Maybe, there might be a drone circling." Mark said, "I am putting in my air buds, keep me informed."

He reached into the glove compartment and took out the pistol checking to see if there is a round in the chamber, then grabbed the four magazines and got out of the car, stuffing the gun in his waistband and the magazines in his pockets then and slowly made it up the hill, watching closely for anyone in the bushes. He got to the yard and tried to run to the corner of the garage, the door security pad flashed, and Alex said, "Be quiet, the garage door opens to a hall there is the master bedroom to the right, the laundry and bathroom to the left, straight down the hall is the kitchen, which is connected to the living room, I just hope he didn't rent it out." Mark slowly opened the door to the house. He could hear the TV playing, he pulled out the gun and had it in front of him, and he crept silently down the hall looking in the rooms. He got to the kitchen and saw a young man tied with four ropes his arms outstretched and his legs apart. He looked like hell.

Everything went very fast. Mark stepped into the room, a man jumped up pulling out a gun, Mark shot him in the forehead, the man behind the camera turned and looked Mark shot him in both shoulders, he went down. Mark yelled at the boy, "Is there anyone else?" Lance yelled, "No, untie me." Mark was assessing the situation; he stepped over to Lance and untied one hand. Lance quickly untied himself. Mark walked over to the man, who was bleeding out on the floor, he said, "Ok I need some answers, and then I will call an ambulance."

A shot rang out, glass went flying, and the man on the floor took a bullet to the chest, a couple of seconds later you could hear the dirt bike fire up and start running through the gears. Lance tried to run but fell on the stairs he went up on all fours, he got to the gun cabinet and pulled out a 308 put one cartridge in it and rested it on the windowsill, he was trying to calm down his breathing then the bike hit the open part of the road a half mile away, he squeezed off a shot, the bike went down with the driver, both hit the road and rolled and slid straight off the corner of the road.

Mark was on his phone calling a cleanup crew, he gave the address. Lance said, "Tell them to pick up the bike down the road." He picked up his phone from the desk, then took the camera off the laptop, and unplugged it, he looked at the phone it unlocked it and he said, "Call Alex." Alex answered saying "Lance what have you got yourself into?" Lance said, "Listen; I need you to trace my internet stream; that is where they are holding my dad." Alex said, "On it, whoa you were being tortured, it leads to Amazon, then to a farm in Alabama, then to a server in England." Lance said, "Can you rerun some of the data to make it look like I am still here?" Alex said, "Good idea, but there is a gap in the feed. I hope they don't see it." Lance said, "Warn the Don, get Rose to safety, they know about her."

Mark asked, "You are Lance the son of Doctor Adam Johnson, and they were holding you to get your father to work on the laser." Lance said, "we have to call the police, and FBI." Mark smiled and said, "You're right we have to go do not worry everything has been taken care of." Lance said, "This has been hell, what are they doing with my father?" Mark said, "The world is being held ransom, your father shot down a satellite and sunk a Chinese aircraft carrier, killing everyone aboard." Lance said, "My father would never do that." Mark said, "Well he did, we need to get out of here."

Alex popped up on Lance screen and said, "I have talked with the Don, hey Rose, Alex here, we need you to go into protective service for a while, the Don is going to send a couple of guys to escort you, the password is braunschweiger, do not go with anyone without the password, and Rose go out your door and to the left, quickly now, go onto the gaming floor. Tony you see her, do you know those guys?" Tony said, "Yeah they have worked here for years." Alex said, "You're right, Sam has been there for 21 years, I think someone has bought him, no Rose turn right go into the hall, I will shut the fire doors, then double back, there are two guards coming through the floor."

She followed his directions and stepped onto the floor by the blackjack tables, two guards stepped up. She said, "What's the password?" The man said, "Braunschweiger." She said, "Let's go." Alex said, "Take them toward the lady's room, and take the second door to the right, it is unlocked." Mark said, "How does he do that?" Lance said, "He put in the security system, it's a long story." Mark said, "I am Mark Neal by the way, you are Lance Johnson, son of Doctor Adam Johnson, we need to find your father." Lance looked at him and said, "Go up to my room and get me some clothes and we go to Vegas to get my sister to safety."

Mark said from the stairwell, "In the morning," he went up and grabbed a shirt pants and a pair of running shoes, he came down and handed them to Lance and said, "We have to get you to a doctor, some of those cigar burns look infected." Lance looked up and said, "There is nothing here; let's go." Mark said, "Get dressed and let me take a look around."

Mark pulled out the man's wallets and went through them, pulling out the cash, he walked over and took the other man's wallet out of his pocket. Lance said, "So you're robbing them?" Mark said, "I need to get to an ATM, I am burning though a lot of cash, these guys look like a couple of regular Joes, the cleanup crew will do a good job it will look like nothing ever happened here, do you mind if they upgrade? They don't have to match exactly what you have if it is easier." Lance said, "Whatever let's go, we have to stop at the house first." Mark said, "There is nothing there and they are watching the place." Lance asked, "What is wrong with you?" Mark said, "Bad back, I think it is arthritis."

Lance said, "I will drive." Mark said, "Oh hell no," they got into the car and in an hour, they were pulling up to Lance's house. Lance pulled out his phone and asked, "Are they watching the house?" Alex said, "The FBI has been watching it since your dad went missing, but I don't think they are the only ones, it should be clear, they did a clean sweep after Mark was there this morning." Mark said, "This car isn't bullet proof; the last time I was here I was in a company car." Lance said, "We are taking the Lincoln; it has been armed."

Mark pulled into the driveway, Lance opened the garage with his phone, and said, "Park in front they can pick up the car here and grab your luggage." Mark said, "But there is no car in the garage." Lance got up and gingerly stood straight; he looked over to Mark and said, "I need a massage." Mark struggled to his feet and to the back of the car to get the luggage, they went into the garage and shut the door then into the house to Lance's room. Mark said, "See there is nothing here." Lance said as he was packing a backpack with clothes, "Shut the door."

He put his hand on the bed frame and the floor lifted the bed to revile a staircase, he said, "Quickly, the game is afoot, I never really understood that saying." Mark said, "Wow I am impressed." Lance said, "I am driving," they walked a hundred yards or so into a huge cavern, and they walked to the workshop, there sat a big old Lincoln town car. Mark asked, "Is this yours?" Lance said, "Bought and paid for, that small satellite in the corner paid for all of this." Mark said, "Was that a live stinger missile we just walked by?" Lance said, "We have to go; Boris is the car armed?"

A small robot came rolling over and said, "Order 7734 has been completed sir." Mark said, "Artificial Intelligence, I don't trust those guys." Lance said, "They are not guys, they are machines." Mark said, as he put his luggage in the trunk, "There's not that much room in here." Lance said, "I know, it is a work in progress, she is a lead sled, it grosses out at 11,455 pounds, we made it into a hybrid so the gas mileage is around 16 mpg."

He walked over to a wall he said, "Boris show Alex." The wall illuminated to show Alex sitting in Pajamas with three screens going behind him, he said, "The car that was down the street moved up, and there is a guy in the apartment across from you with binoculars." Lance asked, "How is that search for the old man going?" He opened an aluminum briefcase, took out an I-phone and touched his old phone with it. Alex said, "It is going slower than I thought, in Iran they have a WIFI controller that is scrambling the signal, I need boots on the ground, and we don't have any. I am working on it, I am thinking it is ran out of the country on fiber optic." Lance said, "Can you run Bob?" Lance said, "I am in house arrest as it is, you want me in prison?"

Lance asked, as walked toward the door, "How is Rose, and do you have protection?" Alex said, "On the way, tomorrow morning, this is what the CIA is sending, you are getting this guy, and they are sending you to Mississippi and Rose to California." Lance said, "So that's not going to work, I am working the field until you get out of jail." Alex said, "They are entering the house; you have to go." Lance said, "Fix this Alex, and Mark, I am driving."

Mark said, "This should be interesting, and how did he know where you were being placed?" Lance said, "If he could find out Spectre can, Rose is not safe." Mark asked, as soon as he got into the car, "What do you know about Spectre?" Lance said, "It was a European mob, they put it down but didn't kill it, it is like an infection it spread through the world and nobody took notice, that is why they are using old spies, they don't know who is infected, the armed service is full of loyal Spectre operatives."

Mark asked, "So how are we getting out of here?" Lance said, "Put on your seatbelts," he touched a button and the car started, he said, "Spy mode, color of car black," the car turned from gray to a glossy black. Mark said, "Now that's cool, so the car is computerized." Lance said, "Roxanne, this is field agent Mark Neal." The car said, "Agent 666 you have been loaded into the system." Mark said, "Now how does it know that?"

Lance said, "Street level please, and Alex is working, if you are wondering why he is under house arrest, his parents came home early and found one of those stinger missiles in their garage unassembled and a small fission trigger, they thought it was a nuclear bomb, my God that was a shit show, they never asked, where the other five stingers were, he is a good friend, and never cracked."

The car rose up into a garage the door opened and Lance pulled out nice and slow. Mark asked, "Do you even have a driver's license?" Mark said, "I have driven Indy cars, tanks, forklifts, dozers, I have a pilot's license, don't worry about me." The car said, "You have a tail, the black Mercedes C300 coupe has made the same turns as you." Mark said, "It could be a coincidence, is this thing bullet proof? It sure rides nice." Lance said, "Bullet proof, bomb proof, waterproof, but it is too heavy it doesn't float, goes right to the bottom." Mark said, "Where are we going." Lance said, "I have a jet waiting we can't use the Tacoma airport; they will be watching that."

The car said, "There is a Porsche 911 following the Mercedes." A large truck pulled up alongside of them. Mark said, "Don't let him cut you off." Lance pushed a button, the middle console opened, he said, "Take the magazine with the blue bullets and shoot that trucks engine. Roxanne slid the passenger seat all the way back and open the sunroof." Mark pulled out a huge gun and put the clip in it holding the blue bullets, he stood and shot one round into the truck's engine. He sat back down and asked, "What the hell is this?"

Lance smiled and said, "A desert eagle 50 caliber, with armor piercing bullets, he gave it some gas but there was a car ahead of them, Lance did a quick turn up hill, the car jumped to 60 miles an hour in a short stretch the Porsche was right on his ass. Lance yelled "Eat trunk bitch," as he slammed on the brakes. The Porsche tried to stop but it was to close and the Lincoln stopped a hell of a lot faster. Mark was thrown into his seatbelts, he said, "It's a mid-engine car that is not going to do anything." Lance had the Lincoln to the floor in reverse pushing the Porsche into a car up over the curb across a lawn into a house. He threw it into drive and said, "There it's a compact, we have to make it across bay bridge."

Mark said, "This isn't going to work, they know who you are, let's dump the car and take an Uber." Lance flew down the road, and said, "This thing is a tank, we just have to make the airport, Roxanne change the lights please." Mark said, "Like that's going to work." When they got within a block of a light it changed to green. The car said, "The C300 Mercedes is following us." Mark said, "You're not going to shake them."

As Lance pulled around a semi-truck Lance said, "Roxanne turn to white color now." Alex ghosted on the windshield, and said, "Get over and take the Treasure Island exit, I have a Coast Guard helicopter warming up to give you guys a ride to the airport." Lance said, "Shall we see if we can make this exit?" He put on his directional on and started to squeeze over. Roxanne said, "The C300 Mercedes is making the same correction."

Lance said, "Arm the EMP." Mark said, "You can't use that here; you will create a huge traffic jam." Lance said, as soon as he got onto the exit, he said, "Fire EMP on the C300 now, see we have narrowed the Electromagnetic Pulse into a twenty-foot corridor, that should fry every computer board in that car." Mark said, "EMP doesn't work on all cars." Lance said, "Concentrate the pulse, it will strip paint off a car, even melt the windshield, I should show you the video, you could cook with it; we took a half a beef."

Alex ghosted on the windshield and said, "Take the next right, code is 'Alex sent me'." Lance pulled up to the gate house and said, "Alex sent me." The gate slid open, Lance said, "Alex is pulling strings, I hope he doesn't get in trouble." Mark said, "Who is that kid?" Lance said, "He is my best friend, we have traveled the world together, you just have to know how to work your parents, my dad is easy, his parents not so much." They pulled up to a landing pad and got out. Mark was still having trouble standing straight, he grabbed his luggage and Lance grabbed his briefcase and backpack. They got to the Coast Guard helicopter and said, "Let's go." The Pilot asked, "Where?" I don't have a flight plan." Lance pulled out his cell phone and showed it to him.

He looked down and said, "Someone just loaded it, we are clear for takeoff." Mark said, "Your friend loaded the flight plan on the Helicopter." Lance said, "That really isn't that hard, is he better at computers than me? Well yes he is, we built a really good one two years ago, it worked really good, too good, we were sent away for a year, for training we went to Japan and learned the art of Karate, Nippon-Kempo, Judo, and Shurikenjutsu. We dug up some stuff on the place and the teachers, and went on a two week vacation to Amsterdam, good times."

Mark said, "How did you do that? Also, the Lincoln just left." Lance said, "It is all deception, smoke and mirrors, and the car can find its way home." The pilot said, "We will be landing, at Hayward Executive airport." Lance said, "We have a private jet fueled and waiting for takeoff, I know a guy that knows a guy that owes me a favor."

Chapter Eight: Vegas

They landed a golf cart ran over to the helicopter and picked them up and took them to the awaiting jet. Mark shook the pilot's hand and said, "We are in a bit of a hurry; we don't want to be late." Lance asked, "You have the flight plan, we have to get going, once we are at cruising attitude please dim the lights, I could use a nap." Mark said, "Great idea, the last two hotels rooms I didn't get to sleep in and the night before that I was in a river." Lance asked, "You were where?" Mark said, "Nothing, it has been a long three days."

Lance said, "You're telling me, so bring me up to speed, you were at my Dad's work up in Oregon, you went to Chicago, what the hell were you doing in Chicago." Mark said, "I found a clue, Chicago the Safe House." Lance asked, "Did it say, The Safe House or a safe house there is a big difference, if it was The Safe House, you weren't even close." Mark said, "We get your sister and put you and her in protective custody." Lance said, "Whoa there, we are going to put Rose in protective custody. Alex is setting that up, I am coming with you to The Safe House to get that clue, I have to find my father."

They both took a nap and the pilot said, "Landing in 36 minutes at McCarran airport Las Vegas." Lance said, "Oh I am stiffing up; I hope everything is set for tonight." Mark asked, "What stuff?" Lance said, "I need a shower and a bed, five hours of shut eye, we have an early flight at 5:00 A.M.." Mark said, "What, where are we going?"

Lance said, "We have a meeting at The Safe House, and are going to talk to the mob? Speaking of the mob I heard you had a chat with the Don, oh and I watched you get shot twice in the back, you know if they would have hit your spine you would be a cripple, it would have shattered your vertebras and tore up your spinal cord." Mark said, "How did you see that?" Lance said, "Vegas baby, you're always on camera, here let me pull it up the camera was high definition, watch it in slow motion frame for frame watch as both bullets hit." Mark said, "Wow that is something." Lance said, "That is one hell of a shirt, does it come in Hawaiian print? Really. I need something like that.

"Alex are you listening? I guess not." Mark asked, "Should I order an Uber, or do you have that taken care of?" Lance said, "Everything is taken care of; this isn't my first time to Vegas." They left the plane and went through security with their luggage, walked out the door and down a row of waiting vehicles and there was one with a sign Lance Johnson. Lance said, "This would be the one." Mark said, "Agent 455." The man took the luggage and put it in the trunk, once in the car he said, "666, I thought you were dead." Mark said, "Nope just retired, I am Mark Neal, Private Eye."

Lance asked, "Do you have something for us?" The agent handed back a plastic bag, then another. Lance said, "I took the liberty of getting you a 45 colt 1911 something old fashion, you have three clips. I myself have a small five shot XDS Springfield 45." Lance started to take off his shirt, and put on the shoulder holster, he said, "I would have got you one but I am afraid you couldn't have worn it."

The driver was driving down the strip and asked, "Front or back." Mark looking at the huge pyramid said, "Front it is much closer to the check in." Lance said, "We have a meeting and we are going to have to walk all the way through the casino, this place is huge." Mark said, "You're telling me, I was just here." Lance said, "You're right, I have reservations for two rooms, all we have to do is pick up the keys."

The driver pulled up underneath the Sphinx and got out. Mark said, "There is something about Vegas." Lance said, "It's the architecture. I mean look at this place, and the Excalibur, it's a castle, just down the road is the Eiffel Tower, the first time I was here it was magical, I think I was eight I spoke at an environmental seminar, they didn't listen, so I built a company making bioplastics."

Mark asked, as he took his luggage, "So how is that going for you?" Lance said, "Running a company is not my thing, I sold 48 percent it is still running I think I made 8 million last year, we are putting most of the profits back in, it has to boost the production." Mark held out a fifty to the agent and said, "Stay safe." The Agent said, "You too my brother."

As they were walking in the casino, Lance said, "Now he checked out fine, but how do you know if he is dirty?" Mark looked at him and said, "What do you mean, you think he is Spectre?" Lance said, "We have looked into his bank accounts, nothing out of the ordinary, but how can you be sure?" Mark said, as they stood in line, "Anyone here could be watching us." Lance said, "To the check in," they stood in line for five minutes Lance said, to the woman that was doing the bookings, "You have rooms 204 and 205 reserved for Lance Johnson and Mark Neal; all we need are the keys." She said, as she handed over the key cards, "Your meeting is at 5:00 in the main office." Mark said, "Facial recognition software, they know we are here." Lance said, "Oh yes, we put in the security system, one of the best in the world. Let's get cleaned up and get to the meeting."

A half hour later Lance walked to Mark's room and got him for the long walk to the meeting, he said, "It is at the Don's place." Mark said, "Tony Breakers apartment, very nice, I was just there." Lance said, "I believe in Lombardi time, if you aren't 15 minutes early you are late."

They walked up to a door and it opened to an office room with a girl behind a desk, she said, "He is waiting for you, go right in." Mark smiled and said, "Thank you." They walked into Tony's apartment; well, the front room was more like an office. Lance said, "The Don, I am so glad you took care of my sister Rose, where is she? " Tony said, "First we take care of business, what are you going to do with her, she is under contract?" Lance said, "We will keep in touch, this is more like a vacation, a week maybe two, you have heard they have my father." Tony said, "Yes I know about that, there is a reward on information of his whereabouts."

Lance smiled and said, "I will double it, we are grasping at straws here." Tony asked, "Your friend Alex he doesn't know." Lance smiled and said, "Just give him a few days." Tony said, "Agent 666 I am surprised you are still walking, I watched you get shot frame for frame that was one hell of a shooting." Mark said, "I would like to thank you again." Tony said, "Don't think of it, and by the way those hit men didn't know anything."

Rose walked into the room, she said, "Lancelot what is going on?" Lance walked around her and said, "You look nice as a brunette, but I thought you were supposed to be dressed as a country girl." She smiled and said, "I will change, Tony likes it when I dress, was this your idea, the fake tattoo and it is even on my drives license." Mark said, "I am glad you are safe; we are going to put you in protected services for a week." Lance said, "Alex will be putting you in protective service, hey Alex you out there?"

A screen on the wall illuminated he was still in his pajamas, he said, "Rose I would rather you blonde, I hope you don't mind spending the night with Mark he has two queen beds, tomorrow morning Brent this guy, they wanted to stick you with Mary but you would look more normal with a guy, he is going to be your boyfriend for a couple of weeks." She said, "I have a show to do, and when did you get to pick my boyfriends, and you put 155 pounds on my driver's license and made me two inches shorter."

Alex turned the camera to show a short video of a large man putting out a cigar on Lance's chest and said, "This could be you; these guys are playing hard ball." She looked at Lance and asked, "They tortured you." Lance said, "Just to keep Dad working, I have to find him, so we need you out of the way, are you packed?" She looked at Alex and blew him a kiss and said, "Love you." Alex blushed and said, "Not the way I would like, I love you too, listen to the guys they are there to keep you safe, and leave your phone with the Don." She looked at Lance and said, "What?" Lance said, "He is right, they can track that phone anywhere on Earth, Mark give her the burner phone I gave you and you had better put Alex in it too."

Alex said, "Take Mark to his room, get something to eat, then to bed. You have a 6:00 A.M. flight." Lance said, "It's a 5:00 A.M. flight." Alex said, "I changed it, you guys need some sleep, they are flying coach, you get first class and you meet up with Brent at your destination, he seems clean." Mark asked, "Did you change that too? This is my case."

Alex said, "Simmer down, take Rose sorry Julia." Lance said, "The Julia Robinson, Rose you should be proud Julia solved Hilbert's tenth problem." She held out her hand, Mark took it, she said, "They are always doing something weird; what did you change his name to?" Lance said, "No he is already dead, they had him scrubbed from the system, now get going I will meet you at the airport, please don't be late."

The two of them left the room and Lance looked at Alex and asked, "So did you find him?" Alex said, "I am still stuck in Iran, I am thinking they put a camera on a screen and did the change low tech so it is hard to hack." Tony asked, "What are you trying to do?" Alex said, "I am tracking the video stream from Lance's cabin, which has gone cold, they hopped from server farm to server farm across the globe, then ended in Iran." Tony asked, "Did you ever think he is Iran?" Lance said, "He could be right, maybe it just ended there." Alex said, "No, well maybe, this is just a hypothesis, I need concrete proof to make it a theory."

Lance asked, "Tomorrow; do you have the meeting set?" Alex said, "Everything is set even the Bear will be there." Lance sounded excited he said, "Really, I haven't seen Boris in a long time." Alex said, "Everything is ready for tonight, should I tell her you will be there in an hour?" Lance smiled and said, "That's a big ten four good buddy, how is getting out of house arrest going? I put in a good word."

Alex said, "I really don't mind much; I can do more here than you can do in the field." Lance turned to Tony and said, "Again I thank you for everything you have done for my sister." Tony said, "I should be thanking you she is very talented; she sells out the show every night so keep her safe." Alex asked, "Do you have any problems with the security? If you do just give me a call."

Lance power walked to his room and pulled out his briefcase and put on a disguise, a wig, glasses, tight gloves that looked like old man's hands, you could see the veins a couple of small scars, the face mask was cast off of his face. This was Hollywood quality and changed everything about his face, different eyebrows, nose, chin, a stubble beard. He used makeup to blend in around the eyes and neck, and then he put on a wedding ring.

He packed everything and headed to the door with his briefcase and his backpack. When he got to the door he said, "Ok Alex make me disappear." He stepped into the hall; Alex wiped him from the video until he got into a crowd. Alex said, into his air pods, "You're live, enjoy the nurse." Lance smiled and walked out to the valet and said, "I need a cab." The man raised his arm and a cab came pulling up Lance said, "The Rio casino." The man asked, "Front or rear?" Lance said, "Front please, and do they still have the Pen and Teller show playing?" The driver said, "I have no idea it has been years since I have seen the show there." They drove down the strip, Lance watched all the people moving about, the fountains of Bellagio, the volcano at the Mirage, soon they reached the Rio.

Lance walked in went up to the counter and said, "You have a room for Henry Rose, and has my wife gotten here yet?" The man said, "No she hasn't." A girl in her twenties wearing a nurse's uniform came up behind him and said, "Hi honey did you order a nurse?" Lance said, "Yeah I guess I did, I sure could use one, I am getting the key now." The man behind the counter said, "Really? Who did this to him?" Lance said, "So we are into role playing. Are you jealous? Just get me the key." He said, "And here you are your premium suite, over 500 square feet it comes with two queens, floor to ceiling windows with a strip view."

Lance looked into the nurse's eyes and said, "I have missed you, come, let's go to our room." She asked, "Are we going to see Penn and Teller?" Lance said as soon as they got into the elevator, "No this is a one night and I need sleep, Penny I have missed you so much, how are the husband and kids?" She said, "It's the boyfriend and kids, everything is going well, I can't thank you enough, and Alex had me stop at Walgreens and pick up some weird shit." Lance said, "Kind of kinky; hey I want you to play nurse; I will show you in our room." He picked her up and kissed her on the neck, he said, as he licked her earlobe, "Oh I need this, and it hurts."

When they got into the room, Penny hit a button and the drapes opened and music stated to play, she said, "Hey even the smaller suites have this." Lance said, "This is a premium suit, our usual suit but not that much smaller," he took off his shirt showing her his back, he said, "I just need bacterial spray, I don't need infection setting in." Penny said, "Oh my God what happened to you?" Lance smiled and said, "I forgot the safe word, let me take off my face, then you can work under me." Penny gingerly touched him and said, "My poor baby." Lance said, "Give me five minutes; find me a wall with nothing on it." Penny said, "Found one, it isn't a whole wall." Lance came out of the bathroom with one of his hands off, he pulled out his phone and said, "Alex could you video chat with Penny for a minute and give me an update?"

Alex's picture shown on the wall, he said, "Hi Penny, did you pick up the supplies?" She said, "Have you seen his back? Whoever it was whipped him and burnt him." Alex said, "Yes I have seen it, that is why you are going to play nurse, after you shower him, use the silver sulfadiazine on the burns, and on the whip, marks use the trimethoprim-sulfamethoxazole, and if you look into your bank account you have already been paid the customary ten grand." Penny looked into the camera and said, "You know I miss you too."

Lance said, from the bathroom "Maybe after this we can sneak out here for a weekend, what do you think?" Alex said, "That would be great; the last time the three of us were in Vegas was a great weekend." Lance said, "Mind if we order room service, here let me have the camera, do a strip tease for Alex." Alex said, "You know you have to get your butt moving, order a meal and get this boy ready, he has a wakeup call at 3:00 A.M., and a flight at 6:00 A.M. so get going."

Penny said, "You heard him get undressed and let me wash you." Lance chuckled and said, "I don't know who you were listening to, but he said order dinner then shower, I have to carefully take off this mask and have everything ready to put it back on in less than eight hours." She said, "Don't you have another one? Last time you ripped it off." Lance said, "Yes I do but this time it is different." Penny asked, "Are you going to tell me what is going on?"

Lance said, "This doesn't involve you; we are playing hardball and people are going to get hurt. I am going to have the chef's tasting from the Voodoo streak joint, you remember up on the 50th floor, it's $110.00 but its' three courses, let's see I looked at the menu on the plane I will have the Caesar salad, the 6oz surf and turf, and for desert what was that oh the Forbidden Apple, and I would like to change out the whipped potatoes for Lobster Mac, and a Crown Manhattan, unless you would like champagne?" She smiled and said, "I would much rather go up and eat at the restaurant." Lance said, "Not this time, you're going to be back in the room by nine, I haven't been sleeping well lately."

Penny said, "Why don't we do this? If we aren't going to have a proper sit-down meal, we can go to the Carnival Buffet and eat around the world." Lance said, "That we can do, that should be a half hour, did you bring a set of clothes? By the way you are super cute in the nurse's uniform, why don't you put that back on?" She said, "You are getting good at the disguise thing, is Henry your only alter ego?" Lance said, "Henry has been getting me served and laid for two years now, it's not that easy to get the driver's license and a passport."

She smiled and said, "That's right, you can't drink at the buffet, because you are underage." Lance rolled his eyes and looked at her and asked, as he turned on the shower, "Is there anything starting to look infected?" She stepped back out of her nurse's uniform and asked, "So you want me to wash you first? I thought we were going to eat," she stepped into the shower and asked, "You don't want me to scrub your back all the scabs will come off." Lance said, "Be careful we will wing it."

He stood inside the shower than straightened up leaving out a sigh, Penny stepped in behind him and used a washcloth and washed between the whip Mark's and around the cigar burns. He turned to her and took the washcloth and suds it up and washed her from neck to toe and back, the shower took a little longer than it should have. They stepped out onto a towel that was on the floor. She patted him dry and had him lay face first on the bed and asked, "Now is the Silver sulfa whatever is for the burns right?"

Lance said, "That would be the stuff, so how does everything look back there?" She sat naked riding his butt trying not to out to much weight on him, she started to applied the cream, and said, "Some of the burns are quite deep, I think you need to see a doctor, they look like they are healing well, and you can tell the old ones from the new ones, this was done over some time, the old ones don't have the red inflamed look, why did someone do this to you?" Lance said, "Long story, one you will never hear." She had him roll over and did his front, and this took a lot longer than it should have.

When they were done Penny took out a short dress out of her medical bag and got dressed to go down to eat. Lance called Mark and asked, "Did you give Julia the phone yet?" Rose said, "No he did not." Lance asked, "Do you have me on speaker phone?" Mark said, "No she is just really close." Lance said, "Rose be a good girl, you guys need sleep, tomorrow you will be flying United flight 4875, we are going to grab a bite then in bed by 9:00 I suggest you do the same you look like hell."

Rose said, "Who do you have with you, your little girl friend?" Lance said, "Go to bed, and I mean your bed." Penny came out of the bathroom dressed and ready to go down to eat. Lance got up and picked her up and gave her a hug kissing her neck, and said, "I am so glad you are here, let's go." They went down and ate at the buffet it had food from around the world, it was great, Lance got filled in how Penny's life was going, how the kids were doing in school, their trip to Disneyland. They got up to the room, Lance had a Kahlua and cream, he got ready for bed she checked his burns, put on a little more cream, this took a little longer than it should have, he kissed every part of her.

Lance said, "It is almost nine, time for bed, and time for you to go." She asked, "Are you sure, I could spend the night?" Lance gave her a light kiss on the cheek and said, "Do you really want to get up at three to go to the airport?" She said, "Your right, that doesn't sound fun." Lance said, "It takes me a half hour to put on my face." Penny said, "Now you know what women feel like."

Over at the Luxor Mark and Rose got back from there meal, washed up, and Rose was trying to find out about Mark; of course he wouldn't tell her anything. She got in her sexy pajamas and gave him a hug, saying softly "I would like to thank you for saving my brother and for everything you are doing." She tilted her head back and stood on her tiptoes and kissed him. He pushed her away and said, "Hey you're welcome, you do know you are half my age." She purred, "Yeah so?" Mark said, "So I don't need any drama, I am going to bed." Rose asked, "Are you sure?" Mark said, "No, and I am going to kick myself in the ass in the morning, but right now I am tired." They both got in their beds Rose had a different idea; she slipped into bed with Mark and spooned him, saying, "I feel safer with you."

Chapter Nine: Going to the Safe House

Lance got up at 3:00 and put on his disguise; he again was Henry Rose, he got a cab to the airport and met Mark and Rose. He walked up and said, "Glad you got her up." Mark looked at him and asked, "And you are?" Rose said, "This is Henry Rose, Henry Rose this is Mark; by the way what is your last name?" Lance said, "Neal. Did you sleep well?" Mark said, "Is that you Lance?" Lance smiled and winked and said, "See, he isn't so dumb, I am going to get a coffee, I will see you in Milwaukee."

Mark said, "About that, why are we going to Milwaukee?" Lance said, "We will talk in the car, The Safe House is in Milwaukee, we have a shit ton of stuff to do." Rose said, "We have a lot to talk about." Lance said, "I don't know you and don't want to be seen with you." Mark said, "Good idea, Rose he must stay undercover, in this business you can't trust anyone."

She stepped up to him wrapped her arms around him and gave him a long passionate kiss. Lance looked up from his phone and rolled his eyes. He went to get a coffee and a wall street journal, he put in his air pods and talked to his phone every once and a while. Soon they were on the plane, he boarded with the first class,. When Mark and Rose walked by, he gave them a wink, Rose flipped him off, and to his surprise there were no delays; in five hours they touched down in Milwaukee, Wisconsin.

They disembarked and headed down for their luggage, there was a good looking guy holding a sign Julia Robinson. Lance said, "Rose that is Brent, he is

FBI, he was handpicked by Alex, he has a 3.4 grade average, has a master's in computer forensics, one of the top ten in Michigan State University, and don't get attached." Mark said, "How do you know he is clean?" Lance looked at him and said, "You don't, sometimes you need faith." Mark said, "So that's what it is coming down to." Lance took Rose by the hand and said, "Come on, I will introduce you to him." Rose followed Lance to the man. Bent said, "Rose Johnson, daughter of Doctor Adam Johnson." Lance said, "Really is this your first day on the job, you just announced who she is, her name is Julia Robinson, read your sign, Rose this is Brent Logan, his mother is Kathy Tucker, he has two brothers and one sister, last year he made $74,000, he has an apartment in San Jose."

Brent said, "How do you know all of this?" Rose smiled and said, "He knows some really smart people, and Lance don't be a smart ass." Lance asked, "Did you get a phone for her?" Brent said, "Yes, how did you?" Lance said, "Just let me see it," he pulled up the contacts, called his phone and said, "Looks good to me, Rose do not call anyone unless it is absolutely necessary, you got that, this is a clean phone."

The light above the carousel started to flash; Lance went back to where Mark was standing. Mark said, "I don't have him in my data base." Lance said, "Remind me to have Alex update your phone, how much memory do you have." Mark said, "It's a company phone." Lance said, "You're running off the cloud, you could be a leak, Alex pull up Mark's phone and debug it please." Mark asked, "Is he always listening?" Lance smiled when he saw his backpack, then said, "He isn't listening, his computer is, it is listening for me to say his name, and you have a call just answer it." Mark's phone rang, he looked at Lance and took it out and answered it.

Lance took his backpack off the carousel; his was one of the first, because he flew first class, he said, to Mark, "Meet you over by Alamo rent a wreck." Mark looked confused and asked, "Which one Alamo or Rent-a-Wreck, they are two different rental places?" Lance said, "Sorry I forgot; Alamo I own stock in the company." Rose came over with Brent, Mark said, "You are boyfriend and girlfriend, you sure don't look happy to see one another." She looked at him winked and hugged him and kissed him full on the lips trying to get Mark jealous. He just turned and watched a new load of luggage fall onto the belt, when he got his he stepped close to Rose and said, "This is not a game, stay alive." Mark walked over to Alamo where Henry Rose was finishing up on the paperwork.

Mark said, "That was quick." Lance said, "It was done on the plane all I had to do is sign the damn thing, I had to stand in line, we have a Ford Fusion it's a hybrid." Mark said, "I wouldn't have guessed you would get a Ford." Lance said, "We are blending in right, you know how many white Fusions are on the road, it's a comfortable ride and has good gas mileage."

Mark asked, "How far do we have to walk?" Lance said, "No that is not how we are doing it; they will shuttle us to the car." Mark said, "Well la tee da, do you know what you are doing?" Lance stepped out to a van with Alamo on the side, they threw their luggage in the back once inside Lance looked at Mark and said, "We know what we are doing, Alex has boots on the ground in Iran, and we are getting help." Mark raised his eyebrows and didn't say a thing.

They got to the car rental place and a white Ford Fusion was parked right next to the door. Lance said, "Get the luggage I will be right out, Lance was out in less than a minute with a man, he walked around the car marking defects on the car. Once the two of them were in the car Mark asked, "Was that necessary?" Lance said, "Yes, I have had them charge me for a door ding that was there before I rented it," the car rolled away slowly on electric power. Mark asked, "So who are you going to get help from?"

Lance said, "You will see, I have been pulling some strings, this could be interesting," he pulled out onto the highway and just stuck with the flow. Mark asked, "Do you know where you are going." Lance said, "Yeah to a martini bar, I have had some good times there." Mark said, "Its eleven o-clock in the morning." Lance said, "We are going to Marquette College, I got a masters in IT, and a bachelors in Public Administration and in Marketing." Mark asked, "How long were you there?" Lance said, "A year, we skipped out and went to Madison, now that's a party college, we did a semester of stem cell research, and it was groovy, man." Mark said, "Groovy? I am not that old, so you are a smart kid, did you know what your father was up to?" Lance said, "Yes, who do you think put in the thirty second tell, the laser light that beams before the plasma blast? You don't need that, it is a tell."

Mark said, "That is an alignment beam." Lance said, "That's, how do you say, hog wash." Mark said, "I say bullshit, this is a nice city." Lance said, "Ok we are going to do something a little different, he pulled off the freeway down into the heart off the city, he drove up Astor and pulled into the hotel parking lot, the hotel took up the whole block, they got out and took in the luggage, Mark said, "Is this where you always stay when you visit?"

Lance said, "I myself like the Pfister, I like the elegance of an old hotel, this one is just far enough out of the way we can stay undetected." They went into the hotel up to the registration and said, showing the girl his phone, "I need the keys for 656 and 657, they are ready and are paid for." He held out a fifty between his fingers and said, "We are already late, I have to get dressed for a meeting." She coded two cards for both rooms, and said, "I hope you enjoy your stay."

Lance grabbed the key cards and said, "Come on let's move, we have to make this meeting." They took the elevator to the 6th floor Lance said, "I will leave my door open, meet me there." Mark showed up to Lance's room to find him putting spirit glue remover on his wrists, he said, "This will take about four minutes." He started to work around the edges of his wig, and it came right off, he carefully wiped everything off, he folded it nicely, his face, hands and wig, then washed his face and said, "Let's go." They got back into the car and went back on the freeway, for a couple of miles then exited into the university campus to the Ambassador hotel; he said, "This is an old hotel, a hundred years old. I mean the Beatles stayed here; I will park the car." Mark said, "I hope they have a restaurant," They parked close by; Lance said, "At least they only charge $25 a night, California is crazy." Mark said, "I just paid $42 in Chicago, and they charge $62 at the Drake in San Fran."

Lance walked up to the registration and said, "I have two rooms under Henry Rose," he got the keys and found Mark looking at the pastries in the coffee shop, he said, "Come on we don't have all day." Mark said, "We have to eat something." Lance said, "Fine, I will have a café mocha and throw in a couple of extra shots of espresso, and an apple turnover, a long john, and a scone." Mark said, "Really, did you catch that? Hell if I ate that I would be a thousand pounds." Lance walked out to find out when the shuttle leaves, he came back and said, "We have seven minutes may I have my apple turnover now, there so messy the crust flakes off."

They quickly ate and took their coffee on the shuttle. Lance said, "We would like to go to the Pfister, then to the Safe House." They pulled up to the Pfister an old elegant hotel, the driver said, "This is the Pfister hotel built in 1893 by Charles Pfister, the travel channel said, it was the creepiest hotel in Wisconsin, it is haunted." Lance said, before he got off holding a twenty between his fingers, "You would say that you work for the Ambassador, 5 minutes." He said, "You had better hurry."

He ran up to the registration desk, with a fifty and put it on the desk, and said, showing her his phone, "I need the keys for room 1100, and 1101, I have a bus load of people waiting for me, so let's make it quick." She asked, for his driver's license, Lance gave her Henry Rose's license, this one had Lance's picture on it. She gave him the key cards, and he was off at a full run, he got to the shuttle with a minute to spare. He sat and put on his seat belts; Mark raised an eyebrow. Lance said, "There is a method to this madness, there is a great piano bar at the top, floor to ceiling windows, it is called the Blu, and the next stop is The Safe House."

They started moving Mark said, "Even down here in the heart of the city, it's pretty clean, the traffic isn't that bad, how cold does it get." Lance said, "Damn cold, we are talking -20 with a wind-chill of -60 and snow." Mark said, "Well that knocked this out for a retirement place." Lance said, "I thought you were going to retire with your own in Niihau Hawaii; that is a really nice place there is no crime, the locals stay on their side of the island, and that over there is the Rock Bottom brewery, good burgers, if I remember right, they have 12 different beers brewed on site, if you look across the river the Safe House is in that building."

Mark asked, "So what is the password?" Lance smiled and said, "I slept with your mother," then he said, loudly, "You can drop us off here, there's no need to drive down the alley." They got up to leave Lance dropped a five in the tip jar, Mark leaned down and asked, "Is I slept with you mother the password?" The driver smiled and said, "It sure is." Lance said, "They leave little clues to The Safe House, see the sign in the window ESPIONAGE."

Mark pulled out his phone and said, "Pabst Theater, does that mean anything." Lance said, "That is an old 3278 model, why didn't mine go off." Mark said, "This phone is outdated, where is this Pabst Theater?" Lance pointed across the street, "Shall we see, we don't have much time." Mark said, "This is an old place." Lance said, "The Pabst Theater built in 1895, it holds like a hundred shows a year, I saw Gaga there, it holds just over a thousand." Mark walked up to the front doors, he walked along and tried ever door one opened, he waved to Lance they went inside, Mark said, "I need a gun."

Lance said, "Ok I think you are right, follow me." Lance took him to the theater it was a huge place. Mark said, "It is a German opera house." Lance said, "Frederick Pabst bought the opera house it burnt down so he had this built, the Pabst mansion has tours if we had time I would take you there, it's a long tour beautiful house though. Mark, look up the mezzanine, a body, let's take the elevator."

They stepped into the elevator and went up to the top floor and stepped out of the elevator and down the hall to find a woman followed them out into the theater. Mark said, "That is just beautiful, there is the gun man." The woman said, "Well if it isn't 666 the beast, I thought you were dead." Lance said, "Lena, what a small world, you made it." Mark said, "You know each other." Lena said, "This is little Lance; you have grown into a nice-looking young man."

Lance said, "This is my piano teacher, she was pumping my dad for information, she is a double agent, German she works for the Bundesnachrichtendienst, BND for short and we knew all along." She said, "You did, really." Lance said, "That is why dad never married you." Lena said, "So have you kept playing?" Lance looked down at the floor and said, "Not as much as I should." Lena said, "In five months he could play better than I, he has a gift." Mark said, "Ok about the dead guy." Lena said, "About that, I am not supposed to be here, could you call in a cleanup crew?" Lance asked, "Why did you want us here?" Lena said, "I did not leave the clue, I got the clue, came in and found him setup here ready for an ambush."

Mark came up reading his phone then he said, "There is a bounty on his head, he is Harry Long the agency has been looking for him for a long time, why doesn't the computers pick these guys out." Lance said, "Your right they shouldn't be able to fly, unless they have been scrubbed from the system or wear a g78." Mark said, "What is a g78?" Lena said, "It is a high tec thing; it alters your look, to throw off the facial recognition software." Mark said, "I will call it in, there is no blood." Lena said, "Blowgun a dart with curare; he didn't even convulse." Lance said, "Well thank you, we would have been killed if you didn't take care of this." She said, "Yes you would have, well at least old 666 would have, I don't know if they want you dead, I heard they kept you hostage to keep the old man working."

Lance asked, "Were you sleeping with him? He was actually happy when you were there and let me tell you that was rare." Lena said, "It was a job, did I like your dad yes I did, he is a good man, did he ever figure out that firewall thing." Lance smiled and said, "That was mine, and yes did we get in trouble, that was called Bob." Mark said, "You did that, Bob stole all the information from all the counties, it went through all the severs gathering information." Lena said, "The only reason you got caught was you moved a satellite." Lance said, "I didn't move the satellite." She said, "That little Indian boy, Alex wasn't it?"

Lance said, "We are going to be late for a meeting I setup." Mark asked, "What meeting?" Lena slid her arm through his and turned him toward the elevator, she said, "He is looking for his dad, and is cashing in some favors; agents from around the world are going to be there." They got into the elevator and Mark asked, "How do you know these people?"

Lance said, "Well it's like this, dad is a very smart person, he worked with a lot of highly secretive projects, so I had a lot of interesting babysitters, I was sent to London to study etiquette at a boarding school, that is where I met Harry French, aka James Bordon MI6, you know he still sends Christmas cards." Lena said, "Did you know he was a spy?" Lance said, "Yes, what a jerk, but now I know how to properly set a table."

They walked across the street down the alley to a door with sign International Exports next to the door. Lance leaned into Lena and whispered in her ear, "He doesn't know the password." He went in first followed by Lena, he met a man just inside the door and said, "Agent here for a meeting password is," he leaned in and whispered it so Mark couldn't hear. Lena did the same thing, she said, "I too am an Agent and I am here for a meeting," she leaned in and told him the password and quickly stepped into the place she met Lance they stood watching a screen with Mark on it. Mark stepped up and said, "I too am an Agent and I am here for a meeting, the password is 'I slept with your mother'."

The guy looked at him and said, "You what, did you just say you slept with my mother? You sick bitch you." Mark blushed then said, "Ok what is the password?" The guy said, "To prove your loyalty walk around and act like a chicken." Mark peeled off a fifty from his money clip and asked, "Will this work?" The man took the fifty and pressed a button under the desk opening the door.

He walked in to find Lance and Lena waiting for him. He said, "You know you are a Dick." Lance smiled and said, "And you are a fun sucker, I wanted to watch you walking around the room clucking like a chicken." A waitress asked, "Will there be three Agents for this meeting?" Lance said, "Yes, please." She said, "Follow me please." They went through the restaurant there was spy memorabilia everywhere, she sat them at a table. As soon as she left, Lance said, "Let's go." He got up and walked over to a door that said, men on it. He opened it and there was a brick wall, Lance asked Lena, "Three up four over?" Lena said, "I think so, it has been a long time." Lance held his hands on a brick and the brick wall moved, it opened to a steep staircase, Lance said, "It's a thermal lock it senses your body heat." Mark said, "How long has this been here?" Lance said, "Oh boy I know this, it opened in 1966, Agent oh-oh-7 the government backed the place for meetings, and you have never been here have you."

They climbed a steep staircase to a room with five tables, and a small bar in its own room. Lance said, "Zhen I haven't seen you in a long time, and Darwin glad to see you could make it, do you guys know each other?" Mark leaned down and asked, "How do you know Zhen? By the way she goes as Mary Summers." Lance said, "I know her as Mrs. Studder, she was my chemistry, and Darwin is an FBI hacker, so Dar have you been in touch with Alex, have you found Dad yet?" Darwin said, "This is a tricky one, they know what they are doing, we traced it out of Iran into North Korea to the Philippines, they are streaming it to security cameras and to the cloud. Alex has been given clearance to do whatever he can, too bad you dismantled Bob."

Lance said, "That's good it shouldn't take too much time; you are still moving." Darwin said, "It is just the IP address keeps changing. I have never seen anything like it." Lena said, "Here comes Joyce Martin." Lance said, "No that is Susan Richter from Townsen IL, she was a receptionist at my dad's lab, CIA." Mark said, "She made it to Field Agent, her name now is Patty Bottom." Lena said, "No way, Patty Bottom that is hilarious." Mark said, "Now she came in a different door, bypassing the restaurant." Zhen said, "You are the Beast 666 and you have never been here." Patty stepped into the room, she asked, "Mark Neal what are you doing back here?" Mark smiled ear to ear and said, "Just collecting air miles, and how is Miss Patty?" She said, "I hear you have been to the Pabst Theater and left a bit of a mess." Mark said, "I heard there was a bounty on that guy." Patty said, "I looked it up a cool quarter million." Mark looked at Lena and winked.

Zhen said, as she pointed to one of the screens "Oh my God, here comes the Bear." Lance said, "Ah, Pickoffski made it, so you heard of the Bear." Mark said, "He is a ruthless killer; he can snap you right in half." Zhen said, "His signature move is to break someone's neck and place them at the bottom of the stairs to make it look like an accident." Lance said, "Oh I can do that, it's an old Japanese Ninjutsu move, Boris and I had the same master."

Boris reached over and grabbed the man at the reception desk by the throat and lifted him off the chair over the desk. The man's feet were kicking in the air. Lance pulled put his phone and called. Boris switched hands, grabbing him by the shirt, and answered the phone. Lance yelled into it, "Put him down the password is," he cupped his hand over his mouth and mumbled then said, "You better tip him good." Lena said, "That was close."

Lance searched in his phone and found a wall to project onto it, he said, "Ok this is why I call him Bear. I was on a fishing trip to Alaska, let's give you a bit of back story to set it up we were fishing salmon and started up stream to fish Grayling a bear attacked a guide, I wonder if he died, oh well so Boris and I go looking for this bear, it was an old three-toed bear they had trouble with him in the past. We tracked him for a couple of miles, and it started to snow and I do mean heavy, we made a shelter out of brush and pine boughs. We settled in and the Bear came after us, Boris had a Bowie knife strapped to a stick to make a spear, now watch."

He started the show it showed the huge Grizzly bear coming at full speed. Lance said, "This footage was taken with the scope of my gun." Mark said, "Nice scope, it shows the trigger pull in poundage." You could hear Boris yell, "Don't shoot unless you have to." He ran out to meet the bear, the bear reared up on its hide legs, it was at least nine feet tall. Boris lunged at it plunging it spear into its chest, the bear roared, numbers on the scope started to climb, the bear swatted the spear snapping the stick the knife was strapped to. You could hear Lance yelling, "Should I shoot?"

Boris yelled "No," and ducked to miss the huge claws of the beast and dove right into the bear pulling out the knife. Lance kept the crosshairs on the bears head, then you could see Boris on the back of the bear driving the knife into its throat, blood shot out five feet spraying the snow, he then drove the knife to the hilt into the bears ear, the bear went right down. A clap came from the back of the room, a large man stood and said, "I have never seen that, can I have a copy of it?"

Lance took three quick strides and into Boris's arms, he gave him a big hug and a kiss on the cheek. He said with excitement, "You made it." Boris said, "But of course, you need help."

Mark said, "Pickoffski." Boris said, with a weird look on his face "666, I thought you were dead." Mark said, "Just retired." Lance said, "Sit, we have to figure out how to save my father," he walked behind the bar and grabbed a bottle of vodka, a glass of ice and lime juice, and sat it in front of Boris and said, "A gimlet I presume."

Boris looked at Mark and said, "Get Lance here a Crown Royal Manhattan with just a touch of cherry juice." Patty said, "He is just a kid." Boris said, "The fishing trip, he was twelve, and he was the one with the Whiskey, we had a drink, field dressed the bear, and sat around for a couple of hours, in our shelter to keep warm and he pulled out a satellite phone and called for a helicopter to pick us up, I was shocked when he already knew who I was, I mean he was just a kid."

Mark went into the bar and started to make Lance a Manhattan, when he looked at a picture of a golden woman sitting on top of a golden goose, and the numbers 4351594. He went back to the table; they were still talking about the bear. Lance asked, "Did you ever get that skill measured?" Boris said, as he stirred his drink, "It was a big one 26 and a half inches, they figure around 800#, a record killed by hand."

Mark asked, quietly as he handed Lance his drink, "The picture in the bar, the woman on the goose?" Lance said, "Circus wagon, I know where it is." Lena said, "Ok, who knows who is trying to kill the Beast here?" Patty said, "There have been two attempts on his life in the past two days." Darwin said, "There is nothing on the net, and let me tell you Alex is turning over a shit ton of stones. I don't know what kind of operating system he is using but it is powerful."

Lance said, "I have brought you here in hopes you would work together on finding my father, we need to find him and fast and we have less than a week before the next satellite gets blown up." Darwin said, "We don't have much to go on." Mark said, "It is an old German U-boat." The Bear said, "Well just look up German U-boats that were stolen." Mark rolled his eyes and said, "Don't you think that would have been the first thing I did? In fact, it is a VIIC class, there were 568 built in 1938, they must have found one on the bottom of the sea and rebuilt it." Darwin said, "They are slow and can't stay under the water long." Lance said, "We are checking on any nuclear fuel missing and equipment needed to build a small nuclear-powered reactor for a small submarine, it would not be that hard, and the design of the sub is right on with a few adjustments that thing could stay underwater for months at a time."

Patty said, "There are just a handful of subs left and they are all accounted for." Lance stood raised his drink and asked, "Will you help me find my father?" Lena said, "I have my countries backing, we have people on it, I will keep you informed." Patty said, "Anything you need we will get you, this is national defense." Lance said, "Good, they can release Alex from house arrest, let him resurrect Bob."

Darwin said, "Now you know we can't allow that. Bob is just too powerful, it hacked everything." Boris said, "He got caught with a live missile in his garage with a nuclear warhead." Lance asked, "How did you find out about that? It wasn't a nuclear war head, it was a fusion trigger, did they ever find out where it came from or how many were missing?" Mark said, "I keep hearing bits and pieces of this; you have to tell me what is going on." Lance smiled and said, "It's a." Darwin interrupted, "I don't know what I am doing here." Lance said, "You owe me, and I need someone else working a different angle, you really think out of the box." Darwin said, "You do not know to what extent Alexander is going, he has viruses breaking through firewalls penetrating the most secure systems. I think he is releasing Bob." Lance said, "We dismantled Bob, everything will be fine, Alex whatever you are doing your going to have to mellow out a bit, and we don't want to open Pandora's Box." He announced to the room, "Ok Alex is going to keep you all in the loop, do what you have to do, we have been sitting in one place too long." Patty said, "I am supposed to take you into witness protection."

Mark said, "Go I will take care of the boy." Patty said, "That is the fourth man come through the doors that was carrying, I think that job in the theater is getting noticed," she turned and walked out a door behind the bar to Mark's surprise the stairs went up. Lena smiled and said, "I guess it's time." She opened a small door grabbed on to the drawer handles above it and slid down a chute. Mark asked, "Where did the Bear go?" Lance said, "Boris is a big man, but he is smooth, kind of freaky isn't it, come on this way, we come out in a Chinese restaurant, I could go for some Crab Rangoon."

Lance took Mark through the apartment building into the next building and down to the restaurant. They stopped for six Rangoons and a coke. Lance said, "Let's go across the bridge and to the brewery, we need to kill an hour." Mark and Lance walked across the bridge and seen a car pull into the parking lot of the brewery, and three men were coming up the sidewalk behind them. Mark said, "I need a gun, come on." He led Lance down the side of the bridge dropped down to the dock. He yelled to a man on a boat, "We need to use your boat, get on." The man said, "No way; get out of here." Mark said, "Really I will pay for any damage, just go."

Lance through off the lines a shot rang out. The man slammed it in reverse pulling away from the dock and slammed the throttle down the boat jumped to a plane a bullet went through the windshield, another hitting the seat. Mark yelled, "Just take us a couple of blocks and drop us off." A string of bullets hit the water and ran across the bow of the boat as a man in a car fired a machinegun from a bridge. The man flew down the river to be met by another boat this one had a guy in the bow firing a pistol. Lance pointed to a channel; the guy took it. The driver yelled, "This runs out to the harbor, I don't know if I can outrun him, but the Coast Guard is out there."

They were at full speed weaving between other boaters and Kayakers. Mark said, "We have to get off the river any of these bridges could hold a sniper." Lance took out a set of darts from his pocket, tapped it with his phone and locked onto the driver of the boat behind them, and the dart shot straight up then right down exploding when it hit the driver. Mark shouted, "Let's put some distance between us and the burning boat, there are going to be cops all over." Lance said, "There the Screaming Tuna restaurant, go up a half mile turn at the Harley Davison Museum, and pull up to that dock over there."

The man pulled up to the dock, Mark handed him a card and said, "Call this number, they will take care of everything." Lance caught a hold of the dock and held on till Mark was off then he pushed the boat off. Lance made a call, and said, to Mark "Four minutes, the hotel shuttle will pick us up." Mark said, "Really, ok I think we should get out of town; do you know where Mother Goose is?" Lance said, "It is a circus wagon, it is at Circus World, about a three-hour drive, and right now we are going to talk with the mob." Mark said, "The Mob, what the hell?" Lance said, "We are cashing in chips, a lot of people owe us favors, and this is not Spectre."

The white hotel van showed up they hopped on Lance said, "To Maders, now Mark this is an old German restaurant, it was established in 1902, they made it through the great probation, serving food, it has always been family owned, I think it still is." The driver said, "It sure is, they have great beer there, German food: you either love it or hate it."

They stepped into the place it is decorated in medieval lore there were suits of armor, swords, dragons. Lance said, to a waitress who was dressed in ethnic German waitress uniform, "We are here for the meeting with the Camaron." She looked at Lance and said, "Really, well this way," and she led them through the bar area through a dining area to a large room were a dozen guys sat at a table with four guards, standing. Lance said, "I need a plate of Kassler Rippchen, and a boot of Spaten Lager, thank you." Mark said, "Really you're going to eat in front of these guys?" A well-dressed man stood and said, "Lance sorry to hear about your father, what can we do to help?"

Lance said, "Hans it has been a while," he sat a small disk on the table, pulled out a chair and motioned for Mark to sit and said, "This is Mark Neal CIA, I was in town and thought we should chat." Hans said, "We have nothing to do with this." Lance said, "I know, I am grasping at straws, Specter is strong and very secretive. I shall tell you what you can do for me in a minute, so how is business going?" Hans said, "You were right, we are making more money now than ever before, I can't thank you enough."

A waitress came up with a plate with a smoked pork chop on a bed of sauerkraut and a glass boot of beer. Lance stood and motioned to the place where nobody was sitting. She sat the beer and the plate and started to back away. Lance stood and said, "Thank you," as he handed her a hundred, then walked over to the older man. The guards stepped a little closer the old man waved them off. Lance said, "We all know Specter is blackmailing the governments of the World for a trillion dollars, we have a week to stop them from blowing up three satellites." Hans said, "I told you, I know nothing about this."

Boris almost had the plate of Kassler Rippchen gone, and was almost finished with the beer, he said, "Damn good beer." One guy blurted, "Christ its Boris Pickoffski, the Bear." Lance pulled out his phone and looked at it and said, "You're not the one I am asking, this whole thing is smoke and mirrors, I do not know why they are doing this, why they took my father, I mean come on I could shoot down a satellite." Hans asked, "Why are we here, and where the hell did the assassin come from?" Boris stood behind one of the men, and the man's phone started to play Mikhail Glinka, the anthem of Russia, the man tried to turn it off. Boris grabbed him by the shoulder and hit him with the palm of his hand displacing a vertebrate in his back paralyzing him. Lance said, "Phone please."

Boris took the phone from the man's lap and said, "Nice song," and tossed the phone to Lance. He caught it and said, "Alex please," the phone went silent. Lance said, "Hans this phone has been mined, it is unlocked, you can check it for more leaks, the real question is how many more Specter agents are in your hire?" Hans said, "I will be dammed." A guard said, "Sir we have incoming, the police are going to raid this place they are on their way." Lance said, "Time to go." One guard talked to his watch and said, "Cancel the security, open the doors."

Lance said, "Let's slide out the side doors we can go down a couple of blocks to a Beer Garden." They ran like hell out the side door and through the alley to the next block to the beer garden. They got inside to find Boris sitting there with a huge stein of beer. Mark asked, "How the hell did you beat us here?" Boris said, "This is Spotted Cow it's a nice beer, Barkeep two Gaffel Kolsch twelve ounces, they aren't staying long." The bartender asked, for Lance's ID. Boris said with a stern voice looking the guy in the eye, "He is my son."

The bartender said, "Ok then, he handed him the beer." Mark said, "Boris I don't know how you can drink so much beer I would be pissing every ten minutes." Lance said, "Our ride is just down the block, thanks Bear I owe you one," he put the glass to his lips and downed it in like 4 seconds. Mark watched and asked, "Where did you learn that? Come we have to be on the move." As soon as they got out of the bar, he asked, "Do you know how dangerous he is?" Lance said, "Oh that pushing the vertebra against the spinal cord to paralyze someone they have been doing that for centuries, don't they teach you that in spy school? I went to Mad Town for college."

Mark said, "We have to quit using the shuttle." Lance said, "Hey it's free if you have a room at the Ambassador." Mark said, "That's what I mean they will know where we are staying, and you are putting him in danger." Lance asked, "Where is our luggage? So we are not staying there, come on, time to go."

They got on the shuttle and went to the Pfister, up to the 23rd floor they walked past the pool to the Blu Lance said, "It is a nice quiet piano bar," they had a blues band playing nice light blues. Mark asked, "What are we doing here?" Lance said, "We are waiting, let's sit by the window." Mark asked, "So what is the red flame on top of the building," Lance said, "I know this, it is the Gaslight building, built in 1930, the light is a 21 foot glass flame it was added in 1956, the light is a weather beacon, when it is red warm weather is ahead, when it is blue no change in view, and gold is for cold, and here comes the girl we are waiting for, Miss Patty, here is the room key, a bottle of champagne has been delivered, you have a half an hour, find out what she knows."

Patty asked, "Why didn't you go into protective service? We sent a guy." Lance said, "And what would get done? Your people are dragging their feet, that phone we got at Mader's has numbers of Specters Agents, boss's contacts, and each one of their phones has more leads, that was a huge find, we have AI working on it." Mark said, "AI artificial intelligence that can be nasty." Lance said, "I know your last case was with Doctor Moreau, we helped with giving the robots hip action, he couldn't get them to walk right, and they couldn't run at all, did you see the giant scorpions?" Mark said, "See them, we fought them, that is what kill the doctor, and those robots could run like twenty miles an hour."

Lance said, "This is above Patty's clearance, the two of you go down to the room you have a half hour, or I leave without you."

A waitress came up and asked, if they would like a drink. Lance said, "A kiddy cocktail, and make it with diet sprite please and four cherries, these two are going." Lance looked at his watch and said, "A half hour." Mark asked Patty, "Shall we?" She held out her hand and Mark took it. They both left. Lance turned the dial on the face of his watch and pushed it, holding it down until it flashed.

He started to work on his phone, his kiddy cocktail came with four cherries, he pulled out a hundred-dollar bill and said, "Here keep them coming, and can I get some kind of a snack, pretzels, nuts, or something?" He opened six different websites and was face chatting with Alex. Lance asked, "How deep did you get with the phone?"

Alex said, "Well it's not a dead end, he was just a plant, we are going through their phones every call he made and every call he received, then every call they have made and received, we are talking about hundreds of thousands of calls and conversations, give me a view of the skyline, it has been a while since we have been in Milwaukee." Lance turned the phone to show the skyline and the bar.

Alex said, "The Gaslight building it is going to be warm tomorrow, so do you have any clues?" Lance said, "I have more faith in you than the CIA these guys they are fighting an enemy they don't even know who it is." Alex said, "I am making a fishbone graph, it is spread worldwide it started in jolly old England, spread to Russia, then China through the Middle East, it's Worldwide. And let me tell you, if we needed to get a search warrant, I am going to prison for a long time." Lance asked, "Do you have Robbie running?" Alex said, "A little more than half speed, we can't get caught with running Bob, there is so much data, I am mining everything we have stored, and all the storage farms, they are using an encryption that makes them stand out, it is only time." Lance said, "I have sent you a piece of the laser blueprint, the diode is a muv m64, it will create a beam using two trillion watts, that U-boat must be nuclear run with a huge generator."

Alex said, "There are only a few places that a diode that large could be built." Lance said, "I am pulling a bit of power to the home computer can you see it on the grid?" Alex said, "Fire up the generators, you can see a spike, and you have to spread out your search, better yet let me do it, you are going to expose us to the World and we don't want that, by the way where is your babysitter?" Lance said, "I needed some space, I sent him to a hotel room with Patty Bottom, can you believe they gave her that name? I would like to pat her bottom."

Alex said, "Focus on the task at hand, I am monitoring the FBI, CIA, Mi6, KGB, MSS, ASIS, CSIS, DGSE, RAW, BND, SVR, now I know you think that is the new KGB but they are separate, the SVR is working with the Chinese, and the SIS is the MI6 rebranded, some of these are so secretive one department doesn't know what the other is doing." Lance asked, "Now RAW, that is India right?"

Alex said, "You're looking into the diode, India makes a lot of things, but this is a big one. It is specialized, I was thinking about CSIS the Canadians, they are looking through their ranks and are finding out Specter is in their house." Lance said, "The BND have the German's figured out anything." Alex said, "This is top priority, the whole World is trying to stop this, nobody wants to lose satellites, by the way nice blues band, wish I was out in the field with you." Lance said, "I told them I wanted you released from house arrest." Alex said, "I am. General Armstrong called me himself, I can do more here than anyone in the World." Lance said, "Just don't get caught, Mark is on his way, so stay safe." Alex said, "I am a ghost."

Mark and Patty came back to the bar; Mark asked, "So what is our next move?" Lance said, "Glad you would ask that, it's getting late, now the guy and the girl in the table on the other side of the bar is DGSE, they showed up right after Patty showed up." Mark said, "What the hell are the French doing here?" Lance said, "The World is on high alert, all the agencies are trying to stop Specter, everyone wants to clean house but they don't know who is dirty."

Patty said, "Mark here is clean, I just washed him myself." Lance said, "Ok, Patty you leave, take your friends with you." She smiled and said, "I will try; you are going to keep me in the loop right?" Lance said, "You were supposed to be assigned to Rose, now you are switched to me." Patty said, "Are you sure?" Lance said, "Yes, I am sure; I did it about twenty minutes ago." She asked, "Am I your sister?"

Lance said, "No you're my girlfriend." She shook her head and said, "You're just a kid." Lance said, "I am 16, you're 26, and Mark is forty, he could be your father for Christ sakes." Mark chuckled and said, "You know he is right." Lance said, "Stay close, for some reason I need a babysitter, and I promised the General I will keep one of you with me at all times."

Patty gave Mark a wink and said, "Watch your ass." Mark said, "No I will be watching yours." She walked away and Mark just stared at her butt as she walked away. She turned to look at him looking at her; as soon as she left the bar the couple from the other side followed her. Lance said, "Let's make our move, and you are right, we could take the shuttle but we would be putting him in danger, an Uber driver is going to be dropping off someone in about five minutes, we will catch a ride with him." Mark said, "Why do you think it is a him?"

Lance said, "It is almost 11:00 at night, I ordered the ride here is his picture and license plate number, this isn't my first Uber ride." They got into the elevator;

Lance asked, "So what did you find out?" Mark said, "They don't have a clue, Adam your father thought he was working for the Pentagon, a very hush hush project." Lance said, "Well that I know, who is behind it?" Mark said, "You know more then I, hell, you worked on the damn laser."

Lance said, "Calm down, the whole world didn't see this coming, maybe they should just pay the trillion dollars." Mark said, "That is not an option, we have to stop this." Lance said, "And here is our ride right on time," he stepped up to the car and opened the door for a girl, the guy got out the other side. Lance leaned in and said, "I am Lance, your next ride." The driver said, "To the Ambassador."

Lance smiled and said, "Yeah, that would be the place, here is a twenty, lose the blue sedan, it's a private eye, my girlfriends dad has them watching me, for some reason he doesn't like me." Sure, enough as the Uber pulled out the blue car started to follow him, he slowed down to almost a stop than floored it to get through a yellow light went up two blocks turned onto the freeway dropped off at the first exit and back tracked, the driver said, "We lost the blue car but seem to have picked up another, the white SUV should I lose him." Lance said, "No that is fine, I haven't done anything wrong, if you act guilty, they will think you are, this is the first time he has put two people on me, it is his only daughter."

They pulled up to the Ambassador, Mark said, "It has been a long day." Lance said, "That it has, and sir thank you for the ride, was that SUV still following?" The driver said, "Two blocks back, he has matched our every move." Mark said, "It has to be a tail you took him for a ride around the block and through an alley."

Lance said, "Come on old man the night is still young." They went into the hotel and into the bar, Lance palmed Mary the keys to the rental, as he walked by, she was wearing a cropped top and short shorts." She headed out the side door, Lance and Mark got a drink and went to the elevator. Mark said, "I think I saw Zhen Yang."

Lance said, as he pressed floor two, then floor twelve, "You mean Mary Summers, how do you guys keep your names straight? Like you Mark Neal, you just got that name, you have changed names seventeen times since you were an agent." Mark said, "Really, I have never counted and my files are sealed."

Lance smiled and said as they left the elevator on the second, "Alex has been given free access to the net, we had to shut down Bob, come on keep up there were some firewalls that will pose a program but with Bobs AI it figured a way through it, ok downstairs, I have forgotten how big this hotel is." Mark said, "Nothing like Vegas." They stepped out the back door to have Mary pull up in their rental car. She said, "We meet again."

Lance said, "The Astor Please, and could you take the roundabout way? We had a tail on the way here." She smiled and pulled out onto the road, around a couple blocks. Lance said, "Mark if you are on vacation, or just want to kill a few hours, that's the Pabst mansion defiantly worth a tour."

Mary drove up onto the 794 freeway and downtown, twenty minutes they were at the Astor. Lance said, "Shall we have a quick meeting in Mark's room?" They went up to Mark's room, Lance asked, "Are we working with the Chinese or not?" Mary said, "I have given orders to do whatever I have to do to stop the satellite killer." Lance said, "General Bo Vang, that is your boss right, he has given the green light to work with Mark here an hour ago." She said, "That was an encrypted message." Mark said, "That is why they hacked it and I don't think we need her." Lance said, "She is damn cute."

Mary smiled and winked at him. Lance asked, "Can you remotely turn off the tracker you put on the car? We don't want anyone to know we are here and you are staying the night, we both have two queen beds, where are you sleeping?" She said, "Your room, you don't mind do you?" Lance smiled and said, "No I don't mind, but I need sleep we are out of here by 8:00, so you sleep with Mark, and nobody contact anyone, if they know the players that are in the game and will be looking for you online." Lance went to his room and went right to bed it was 1:00 A.M.

Chapter Ten: To the Circus World

At 7:00 Lance called Mark and said, "Good morning, we have to get on the road and get your clue." Mark asked, "Are we bringing the girl? She is a beautiful thing." Lance said, "How close are you to being ready? I will meet you downstairs at the complimentary breakfast in ten." Mark said, "Let's make that twenty." Mary said, into the phone "All work no play isn't any fun." Lance rolled his eyes and said, "In twenty."

He opened his laptop and his phone; he remotely checked his computer at his house that has been running all night looking for anything that would link his father to the laser, and where the parts for it could have been ordered." He said, "Alex are you up?"

Alex came on wearing the same pajamas he was wearing yesterday, "Yeah dude, there are so many variables. I have been looking at the U-boat it is a VIIC class, I have the blueprints. and who has accessed them in the last two years, which is not many people. I have a professor talking to the VZ, he published a small compact generator that would give you the 2 trillion watts it takes to fire your dad's laser. Now we are talking about a multilayer diffraction grafting, with a five-beam amplifier. Now one key part is the driver module, now I figure the doc would have had to use a carbon dioxide refrigerant since it is in a ship, and that has to be controlled, and found a guy doc Rupert Rasmussen from LLNL did you know they moth balled that laser there? It is the largest laser of its kind, way too big to fit in a U-boat." Lance said, "The VZ is Czech Republic, is that Johan Svoboda, he was over for lunch one day." Alex said, "The late Johan, he just took a cyanide pill, how sloppy are those guys."

Lance said, "Check the guards, this Specter runs deep." Alex said, "You're telling me, it is a worldwide organized crime unit, and they keep their ties short, I have been running tens of thousands of hits from that phone, they just keep circling, making it look like a local mafia, and I know it is Worldwide, I keep coming up with cells, Mark just left his room, whoa dude that Zhen chick is hot." Lance said, "Well do what you can and keep me in touch." Alex asked, "What is your next move? And take a tee shirt down for Miss Summers, she looks like a hooker, a mighty fine hooker."

Lance pulled an MIT shirt out of his backpack and said, "Rasmussen, he is the one at Lawrence Livermore in California, I think he is a dead end, he strictly works for himself, pretty stuck up." Alex said, "Now the DND, the Canadians are focused on the diode, everywhere I have gone they have been there first, this is a special made to order thing." Lance said, "I have to get to breakfast, did you break into my notes? I have different prints of the diode, we could get around it with an old solid state stack exchange, it would work better but it would take up some room." Alex said, "I will look into it that, you know that would work, but there again you are talking a lot of heat." Lance said, "You're in a ship there is plenty of water for coolant, when is the last time you slept."

Lance went down to find Mark and Mary eating, he went to the buffet, and sat down a cross from Mary and said, "I brought you a shirt, so in fifteen we head out." Mark said, "I think we should take it easy." Lance said, "The clock is running, and leads are not coming that fast, we found a guy that might have had something and he had a cyanide snack and died while questioning."

A woman came out and sat a café mocha next to Lance and said, "Your coffee sir." Lance held up a twenty and asked, "This is a five shot, mocha, at a hundred and five degrees." She smiled and said, "It should get you going, and how did you say not burn your lips off." The twenty turned into a fifty in his fingers, he said, "Thank you very much." She took the bill and smiled.

Mark smiled and said, "You are smooth, you took an illusion class at The Magic Castle in LA." Mary said, "And you had one on one with Penn and Teller at the Rio." Lance said, "It's all smoke and mirrors, once you learned how it works you can catch it pretty easy, that changing the bill was staged, I don't need to pick up women, so I don't us magic to impress them." Mary asked, "Are you gay?"

Lance said, "No not really, I have swung both ways, but that is a waste of time, I steer away from drama, I have an empire to build, when I am ready for kids, I will find a mate." Mary said, "That's cold, you're young, enjoy life." Lance asked, "What is your definition of life?" Mary said, "Go out and play, have a girlfriend, play ball with the boys, eat hotdogs over a fire, play video games."

Lance said, "I have 46 patents, I have a girlfriend whenever I want to have physical interaction, I have created 4 video games. I have more money than I need, I command respect in many fields, and I have one friend that share the same goals in life." Mary said, "You can never have more money than you need." Mark said, before taking a sip of coffee, "Yes you can, this is not about money." Mary said, sarcastically "So you have over a hundred million dollars?"

Lance looked over to Mark. He nodded, Lance looked over to Mary and nodded. She said, "What the hell am I doing wrong?" Mark said, "Right time at the right place, and don't be afraid of taking a risk." Lance showed his phone to Mark with all Mark's holdings and a grand total of 287 million. He said, "Hey the government doesn't even know that." Lance said, "Mary you make enough money, two hundred grand a year in U.S. dollars, you just spend more than you make."

She looked at Mark; he said, "I know he has friends that are connected, and I never thought Boris also known as the Bear had any friends." Lance said, "I have met him at his house, they sent me to Russia for a month to learn their history. I disappeared for two weeks; sometimes you need to learn by doing, and we had a good time, he taught me many things that were not in any book, we went to Siberia and looked at the effects of global climate change, I wrote a paper on that I was so close to a Pulitzer Prize, I got a A+ and did talks on it there are a lot of things in that permafrost that you don't know, bacteria, viruses, stuff the world hasn't seen in a hundred thousand years and it is defrosting with global warming, good times."

Mark said, "Ok let's freshen up and meet in the lobby in ten minutes, this is a two-hour drive, is Mary coming with?" Lance smiled and said, "She is the only one with a gun." She smiled and said, "You noticed." Lance said, "It is in your bag a Glock 9mm, and a stun gun that would be your lip gloss, your cell phone has one also, it is a model 78w20, made in Beijing by one Jung Lo." She smiled and said, "That's nice to know, all I know if I lose it there will be hell to pay."

Lance said, "You are not just a pretty face, you have had some success at this spy thing you have stolen some top trade secrets, you have even interviewed the chief of staff, your parents are Zhang Wie, and Xiu Ying Wang." Mary asked, "How does he know this stuff?" Mark said, "I have no clue, your records say you were born in San Jose California, went to school in Santa Clare Mission college, and my records have been sealed." Lance said, "I told you if you want your past gone, it will cost you."

They got into the elevator and Lance said, "My God, you have to be kidding me, you are going to turn me over to Patty Bottom, in Baraboo at the circus museum, after I help you get your clue." Mark said, "This is getting dangerous, let's face it you are a kid." Lance said, "Fine whatever; you're not helping anyway, we are just wasting time." Mark said, "Well you say your friend is such a good programmer, he can't even follow a live stream." Lance said, "That was low, even for you, sometimes it takes time boots on the ground, there are many ways to fool electronics, they took us to Iran, Pakistani, Russia, and it was all a deception." Mark asked, "Do you know where your father was held." Lance said, "Well no, the link has been broken; they know we are onto them."

His phone vibrated he looked at it and showed it to Mary, it said, in large letters, "I think she is beautiful." He said, "I thinks someone has a crush on you." Mark said, "Ok how the hell can he see us in here?" Lance said, "He hacked into the security; I even can do that with my phone." Mark said, "No way." Lance said, "It just takes a little time; it is tricks of the trade." Mark said, "I am a freaking spy and can't do that." Lance held up his phone it said, "He is old."

The doors of the elevator opened and Lance said, ten minutes. Mary seductively said, "What can we do in ten minutes?" Lance said, "Ten minutes in the lobby that means you have four minutes to freshen up, and I don't need you to get the clue." Lance packed up while his laptop was booting up, and a spy satellite showed live stream pictures of the hotel, he enlarged the screen and searched the hotel and did a once around looking for snipers. He grabbed his backpack and briefcase and headed downstairs to meet Mark and Mary.

Lance walked into the lobby and said, as he walked toward the door, "Let's do this thing, time is getting tight and nobody is any closer than we were before, this is my dad's life you know." Mark said, "Shall we take it slow? We are going out into an open parking lot." Lance said, "See that's how you grow old in this business; I swept the building and surroundings." Lance's pocket dinged and he looked at it and said, "And Alex swept it with infrared using a Russian satellite that would be a scan using an invisible electromagnetic spectrum consisting of radiation with wavelengths in the range of 750 nm to 1mm between light and radio waves."

Mark said, "I know what infrared is." Lance's pocket dinged, he pulled out his phone and said, "There on to us, the satellite has been compromised, this is good, not they know where we are it is good, we got a hit, Alex had permission to use the satellite, now the Russians are hunting who else hacked it, they have a leak." Mary said, "In other words Specter is operating in their ranks." Lance said, "They have to find someone that is going to cooperate; they just have so many safeguards, so who is driving." Mark said, "I will drive." Lance said, "Fine I will sit in back I have a lot of work to do, I have to plan my next move, and we are running out of time."

Mark programmed his phones GPS. Lance asked, "Did you put it on freeway? If it takes you the closest route; we are going to drive through every small town along the way." Mark turned and looked at Lance and said, "You know this is for your own safety," he looked at his phone and put it freeway mode. Lance said, "They don't know what car we are driving but someone tried to hack the cameras at the stoplights, we have the hackers IP address, and have pinpointed the computer, we have facial recognition, we know who he is and are breaking into his phone, now we are mining, every call he has made we are investigating, he will be arrested in seven minutes."

Mary said, "That's amazing." Mark said, "But if he is good, he would be a thousand miles away, hacking into the computer making it look like he was the one." Lance said, "Nope that is one of the first things you check nowadays, we turned on his camera and watched him typing it into the computer, this is prison time he should sing like a bird."

Mark drove through farmland for three hours and finally pulled into Baraboo a small town nothing out of the ordinary. Lance said, "Drive past it there is parking on the left under the trees." Mary said, "There are a lot of people here." Lance said, "Ah yeah it is a museum, with elephants and clowns, I hope they have the tigers." Mark said, "We are here to get the clue." Mary said, "If we are going to work together you have to keep me informed." Lance said, "There was this dead agent, Jack Brown agent 435 left a clue to this clue, I sure hope it is not a dead end, and why the hell hide it three thousand miles away." They walked across the road Lance took Mary's hand she smiled, Mark gave him a look.

Lance said, "What? She is too young for you." Mark said, "And she is too old for you." Lance squeezed her hand and he said, "You can be my girlfriend until Patty comes, it's always nice to have a girlfriend you know that will stick a knife in your back." She said, "How did you find out about that?" Lance said, "They gave Alex free roam of the internet, once something is on the net it is always on the net, and most of the countries are giving Alex access to their spy network, well maybe not giving, our government gave him free reign, which means I have access."

Mark said, "That I doubt, well Alex might have to go into witness protection after this one." Lance said, "It is throwing red flags around the globe, ok Dad are you buying the tickets?" Mark said, "I am not that old." Lance said, "What do you mean you're 40, that would have made you 24 when you had me." Mark said, "Now you are making me feel old."

Mark paid for the tickets, Lance said, "We should be out of here in a half hour, it has been a long time since I have been here." Mary asked, "When were you here with your dad, I take it?" Lance said, "No I was studying gene splicing at

Madison, went to school for a year, great school, partied a bit more than I should have but still came out with a masters, let's cut right through all this history crap and get to the wagon building."

Lance led them through the building and out the back door across a bridge to the circus, there were clowns, elephant rides, train cars, a big top, Lance said, "This way," they followed him up the hill to a huge building, he turned and said, "A lot of these wagons came from Europe, they are beautiful works of art, now where the hell is Mother Goose?"

Mark said as he walked in the door, "There are 260 wagons here; my God look at that one it has a dragon on it." Lance said, "They all had a job to do, if you ever get to see a circus being torn down, everything has a place, these wagons would be full, a few like the Mother Goose were just for show." Mary touched one and said, "The gold paint is in great condition." Lance said, "Most of it is gold gilding; there it is, sorry that is the old woman in the shoe." Mark asked, "Did they have to raise the wires on the street? Look at this one with the world on it, it has eight-foot swans on it and lions, is that all gold gilding?"

Lance said, "A lot of it is, I just hope Mother Goose isn't in for repairs." Mary said, "I think it is this way, is it a woman riding on a goose?" Mark said, "Yes, it is, that is the one," he walked over to it, turned a dial on his watch, Lance did the same thing. Mark said, "Ok I got it." Lance said, as he looked at his phone and said, "We came all this way for bank account numbers, what the hell this has nothing to do with dad."

Mark said, "I didn't know what the clue was, wait a minute how did you get it." Lance smiled and said, "Timing, you know I couldn't have accessed that file without you." Mark said, "Well let's get out of here." Mary touched the goose and asked, "This is gold leaf." Mark read the sign and said, "It was built in 1886 to 1888 for the Barnum& London circus and is 12' long 6'9" wide and 9'1" high and is gold leaf. Lance said, "A burger and a beer." Mark said, "A burger and a Coke maybe," he texted and mumbled.

Chapter Eleven: Jamaica

Miss Patty Bottom came walking up. Lance said, "That's it, we were waiting for her," he talked loud enough for Patty to hear, "What's taking you so long? You should have met us at the bridge." She walked up and said, "The dog act was funny, I have been here for a couple of hours, Lance we can catch the elephant show."

Lance said, "Come on let's go, we have a plane to catch." Patty said, "Oh no you don't, I am in charge here." Lance raised his arm pointing his finger as he took two steps forward, and said, "No you listen, I am running this show, this is my dad we are talking about, you are going to do what I say and when I say, do you get that, this has been a waste of time."

Patty said, "My job is to babysit you, keep you hidden and safe." Lance said, "You had better keep up then." She turned to Mark he said, "Well you had better go, you could put him over your knee, but he would kick your ass." Lance said, "Come on pick up the pace, you know I really don't need you."

Patty power walked with Lance across the bridge and around the building. Patty said, "I am parked right out front." Lance said, "Do you drive fast? We have to get to Madison, Dane County Airport, it is an hour drive, our flight is in two hours, you had better step on it, pull up to the Ford Fusion and I will get my bags." She asked, "You got the keys?" Lance smiled and said, "I have a phone, and I recorded the signal of the key pod."

She said, "Really, you have to show me how to do that." She pulled up to the car Lance hopped out and was back in within a minute, he said, "Put the hammer down." Patty pushed the car to just ten miles over the speed limit. Lance said, to his phone, "Oh Alex, could you give me a location of the cops on the way to the airport?" Alex came on and said, "You have a free shot to ten miles outside Madtown, there is a state patrol waiting for you there, you had better get rolling." Lance said, "Put the hammer down we can't miss this flight. Alex how did it go with Rose or Julia?" Alex said, "Players are in position, you have a balcony, far enough from the elevators." Patty worked her way through traffic and was moving about ninety down the freeway, she asked, "Where are we going?"

Lance said, "AI is monitoring the airlines, we will stop before the airport and you will change into Joyce Holdor, get it joy asshole." She pushed the car just over a hundred, Lance had his face on and was working on the hands when his phone said, "Slow down, your cop is two miles ahead of you, then you have open road to the airport, so Miss Patty did you bring your string bikini with you?" She said, "Well yes, where are you sending us?" Lance smiled as he said, "We have found my father, well not where he is now, but where he was, we will be there in the morning then we will make plans as we go."

Patty pulled into a McDonalds, Lance said, "Shall we do this quickly? First, let's do the hair, we are going to grease down your beautiful blonde hair, and you are going jet black, with brown eyes, and a lightning bolt tattoo, on your neck, don't worry he sent three of them." Patty asked, "How did you get this stuff; I mean you have been on the move." Lance smiled and said, "Logistics, planning that all it is, now we are going on a cruise, tomorrow we will be in Montego Bay, that is where the live stream was sent, they must have loaded the laser onto the ship and snuck it through the Panama Canal, ok the hair is done."

Patty said, "Really you think that is done." Lance said, "Close enough, now let me put on the tattoo, it doesn't have to be perfect, it goes from just below your jaw under your ear and wraps around to the back of your neck, so if your hair is down, you will not see it." Patty said, "Then why don't I keep my hair down." Lance said, "It's all an illusion; they see the tattoo and don't look any farther." She looked at her driver's license, she said, "Ok I see that, the first thing you look at is the tattoo; your friend did a good job on this." Lance gave her the contact lens, and said, "This is Air Optic, a sexy deep brown, you can leave them in for a week, and we don't have all day." Patty said, "I got my eyes done years ago one of the best things I ever did." Lance said, "You mean your parents got your eyes done?" Patty said, "Ok my parents paid for it, there what do you think?" Lance said, "That will work, God I would love a quarter pounder but we can get a snack at the airport, we are cutting it close."

She pulled into the parking lot at the airport, Lance said, "Long term, it's a longer walk but if they tow the car AI will say you were here, in fact we should have changed the plates." Patty asked, "You're kidding right?" Lance said, "ALPR, automated license plate readers, old technology it started in Vegas, the Casino's used them to track card sharks, they knew you pulled into the parking lot, now they can read thousands of plates on the freeway."

Patty said, "So if they knew I rented this car they can track me without bugging it." Lance smiled and said, "Unless someone hacked into the car rental and changed the plate number in the computer." She said, "So you knew I was come to get you." Lance smiled and said, "The secret service should stay off the net, and every call you have made and text you have written I have read, this is not a game."

They got though security and Patty became Joyce and Lance became Henry again. Lance said, "Shall we find our gate and get a bite to eat, Joy ass." She shot him a dirty look. He said, "That is funny, Alex are you there, yeah that is a great name for her, I love it." She went into the lady's room and came out with her hair done and different makeup. Lance said, "I approve, this is a good look for you, shall we eat a quick burger we have a half hour before boarding, then an hour and a half layover in Dallas, then straight to Montego Bay, we missed our cruise ship, and are going to catch up to it in Ocho Rios."

Patty said, "Why a cruise ship?" Lance said, "I thought I would surprise my sister, she will be pulling into port in the morning, we find the old man and our mission is done, jump on the ship and get a good night sleep, we are cutting it close, and who would have thought he was in the Caribbean." She said, "I thought he was on the U-Boat in the Pacific." Lance said, "You were listening, the video feed was going to Jamaica so that is where we are going and see if he left any clues to where he is." They got onto the plane nine hours later they landed in Jamaica.

Lance sat up most of the night on his phone, Patty looked over to him he smiled and said, "Remind me to take a picture of you in your bikini." She said, "For Alex I take it." Lance said, "Good idea, I will send it to him, did you sleep well." Patty said, "You never really sleep well on a plane." Lance said, "We did really have a breakthrough, those bank numbers, Alex ran them, matched the accounts with who accessed them, this is branching out in a whole different way, we are getting everyone who has been paid, where the deposits are coming from, the whole organization is ran through these accounts, well not the whole just the Americas, and Canada." Patty said, "How much money is in there?"

Lance said, "It flows like a river, some coming in and going out, we are talking billions, hundreds of billions." Patty asked, "What are you going to do?" Lance smiled and asked, "Who do you trust, I don't trust the United Nations, our FBI and CIA are tainted it goes high in the food chain, we know MI6 isn't clean, the KGB is fighting it now." Patty said, "And we thought the British had it cleaned up, it just went underground but why come out in the open now, they had a good thing going."

Lance said, "Greed, money is the route of all evil." Patty asked, "So what is our plan?" Lance said, "Hilton Double Tree, we are going to get four to five hours of sleep, then we are going to drive up the coast in a Jeep, it should be there in the morning, God I hope it is there early, these people are on island time."

They disembarked from the plane the airport was dead it was the middle of the night, Patty said, "Now don't talk to strangers they will try to sell you drugs." Lance smiled and said, "And watch out for the rum punch, they make it with 151 rums, or they used to, that shit will knock you on your ass." They went down and got their luggage and took a taxi to the hotel. Patty said, "This place is huge." Lance said, "Well it is an all-inclusive resort with seven restaurants, let's get to bed and catch some sleep, I booked a room close by."

They walked up to the desk, they were the only ones in the lobby, Lance showed the girl behind the desk his phone she said, "Yes sir: all you need is the keys." Lance said, "I could have programmed them but I didn't have any blanks." She smiled and handed him his keys. Lance sat a fifty on the desk and said, "Thanks, we missed our Cruise Ship, so we will be out of here in the morning." He turned and said to Patty, "I have been here before, my Dad wanted to teach me how to golf, ok he had a conference here, agent 854 was my golf partner, he wasn't bad, we played ten hours a day."

They went to their room, Lance said, "Don't unpack, we take the luggage with us, let me take this face off I would sleep with it, but that is just gross, it starts to smell." She asked, "What bed would you like?" Lance took off his shirt and stood next to the sink he said, "The one closest to the window, hey there is two sinks in here, you can take off that wig." She came in and watched Lance take off his mask, she asked, "What happened to you?"

He said, "Oh that; they wanted to keep Dad working, so they put me in chains and tortured me for a few days, good times, how does everything look back there?" He looked at her in the mirror. She said, "The whip marks are red, but don't look infected, the cigar burns are deep, looks like someone put a few stitches in one." Lance smiled and said, as he slowly pulled the mask off his face and turn back into a sixteen year old boy, "A hooker in Vegas, she did a good job," he handled it with care wiping it out with a washcloth and dried it. She stepped up to the other sink and started taking off the black wig, she said, "Really a hooker, you know I don't look that bad as a brunette."

Lance said, "Yes a hooker a very nice girl we have her on retainer, and you have a very attractive face, it has symmetry that is shown to be attractive in women, you have fuller lips, a high forehead, broad face, small chin, small nose, high cheek bones, clear skin, and wide-set eyes, so yeah you have a beautiful face." Patty asked, "Are you going to be Henry tomorrow?" Lance said, "No, unless we fly somewhere, they will be checking all the airports, we are going to where that live stream was sent." She said, "Oh Alex figure it out." Lance's phone dinged, he pulled it out and turned it on.

Alex's face came up, Lance asked, "When is the last time you showered? He is in the same pajamas as he was three days ago." He looked at him wild eyed and said, "Sleep yes, I have to do that, this is a huge monster you brought to life, the Jeep will be deliver by 8:00 A.M., you have the coordinates of the lab, and show me the girl." Lance turned the camera around and showed Patty washing her face, he said, "She is washing off her makeup; she is staying in character they will be looking for a blonde." Patty dried her face and asked, "Are you really wearing the same pajamas?"

Alex said, "I guess so, there is so much to do and they are letting me run wild, the CIA came in and picked up the parents, I had nothing to do with that, this is an all-out war the whole world is waking up to a secret society living in their houses, Asia and the Americas are separate, this has been done on purpose, we had one small lead into Australia and it is growing, Brazil is mostly ran by Specter." Patty asked, "Are you always listening to us?" Lance chuckled and said, "Yes she is a blonde, his computer is listening for his name, you said Alex and an alert popped up on his screen." Alex said, "So you're in the bathroom together, this usually doesn't happen on the first date."

Lance said, "Good night, and Alex get some sleep." Patty asked, "Is he always this nervous." Lance said, "Did you notice the energy drinks, the pot of coffee, four pizza boxes? He hasn't slept in days, this is his super bowl. We had a system named Bob it was a data collection system it would hack into every server and copy the data, from the whole world everything went well until we moved a satellite to view a nude beach, it happened to be a Russian satellite, they didn't like that then the White House found out we hacked the militaries of the world, I thought we were going to prison for life."

Patty said, "Would you step out while I slip into my pajamas? So how did you get out of it?" Lance smiled and said, "We hacked everyone, and we are the only ones who could access the data, if we dumped it on the internet, it would crash the net and all the secrets would be out there, they didn't have a choice to let us go." She came out of the bathroom Lance was in bed he said, "Sleep, we have a wake up in two and a half hours." She stepped over to him, pushed his hair off his forehead and said, "I am sorry about your dad, everything will work out."

Lance said, "Oh for Christ sakes, I know what is at stake here, I give him a fifty-to-fifty chance of coming out of this alive, and you are really good looking, now get to sleep."

In the morning Lance said, "Its seven o-clock, let's get rolling, I will shower first and go down and see if our ride is there," in five minutes he walked out of the bathroom with a towel wrapped around him, carrying his disguise. She turned on the news. Lance gently put Henry into the briefcase, he turned to Patty and asked, "It doesn't bother you if I change here does it?" he dropped the towel and put on his underwear and proceeded to get dressed. She said, "You're pretty brave." Lance said, "I have read your file, you will do whatever it takes to do a job, my friend is getting you a promotion, you should have a license to kill, and time is of the essence, get your ass in the shower, Joy-ass." She shot him a look, and then asked, "What should I wear today?" Lance smiled and said, "I still need a picture of you in a bikini, oh Alex are you up?" Alex came on; Lance turned the camera on the phone and said, "Here is Patty Bottom in lingerie, pretty sweet, hey."

Alex said, "Wow she is a hottie, you don't have time, we need intel, Mark Neal is on the island, I couldn't follow him, not enough cameras." Lance asked, "Did you get Miss Patty a license to kill?" Alex said, "What oh yes, I have to go." Patty said, loudly, "Take a shower." Lance smiled and said, "You should get a few hours of sleep." Alex said, "Yes must sleep, let me write myself a note, what is she doing?" Lance looked at Patty and asked, "What are you doing?" She smiled and said, "I am assembling a gun, what does it look like?" Alex said, "It looks like you have a nice ass." Lance said, "Put your filter on, you do need sleep." Patty unscrewed a pen and small darts came out, and she loaded them into a small case of blush, that had a lipstick screwed into it making a handle with an eye liner for a barrel.

Lance asked, "Don't you think you should have put on your makeup first." A dumb look formed on her face and she said, "I am going to take a shower." Alex said, "Here's your chance, jump in the shower with her." Lance picked up the room key, and headed for the door, he said, to Alex, "Find Mark, he had to check in somewhere." Alex said, with a Jamaican accent "You are in Jamaica mon, it's a third world, everything isn't connected to the internet, and the hotels that are don't have facial recognition software." Lance begged "It would really help."

Alex said, "Try this, there is a set of tracks that have been added to an under-ground garage, this is a satellite picture five years ago, and yesterday, it runs out on a pier that was built ten years ago, and the live stream went to the house on the hill." Lance said, "That's a nice mansion." Alex said, "They had a big party there last night, there is no parking so there were cars all over."

Lance went down to the desk in the lobby and asked, if a Jeep was left for him. The young man said, "Yes sir, it is parked around the back, would you like it pulled around." Lance smiled and asked, "Is the breakfast buffet serving." The young man said, "Yeah mon." Lance went back up to the room to find Patty dressed and putting on her makeup. He walked up to her and said, "Now we have to look like a couple, can you do that?" Patty said, "How about brother and sister? I am so much older than you."

Lance said, "You are 12 years older than I am, you slept with Mark and he is 19 years older than you." Patty said, "I read your file; you went to Alamo elementary school in San Francisco." Lance said, "Whoa stop right there that is lies all lies, I went to 8 elementary schools, in 4 years, three middle and high schools in two years, I have been to 9 colleges, I have a doctorate in Chemical Engineering, Bio-technology, a couple of Master's degrees, in Computer Science, and some other crap, enough about me shall we talk about you. I have read most of your files and the cases you were on, Alex warned me about getting too close to you, how did he say it, you are a walking petri dish; you sleep with everyone you work with."

She blushed and said, in a pissed off voice "I do not, who said that." Lance said, "Well it is in your files, you will do what you have to, lately you have been given babysitting jobs, keeping people safe, acting security, pushing papers, in fact you have only been in the field for just over three years, would you like to hear what your instructors said about you?" Patty asked, "How do I look, and how do you know this stuff?" Lance said, "You look lovely, I know a guy he sent me a secured file on you, I have your last ten years of tax returns, I don't know who does your taxes but they need to go back to school and ditch the flip flops, this could be a shit fest, we are going to break into a secured place, we think my father had a lab there."

They took their luggage down to the concierge, slipped him a twenty, told him to have the Jeep brought around then went to breakfast, it was a huge buffet Lance pointed out a few things, he said, "Ok it has been a while, this is roasted bread fruit, these fruits are massive their as big as a basketball and hang on trees 50 feet in the air if on fell on your head it would kill you." Patty asked, "And what is this?" Lance said, "Boiled bananas, try the jerk chicken, I am going to get an omelet, and if I remember right their coffee is great here." Patty asked, "You were drinking coffee at 12 years old?" Lance winked at her and said, "I was doing a lot of things when I was 12 years old, I hiked across the Grand Canyon for a school project, climbed Mount Rainier, made my first million."

Patty said, "No way, your dad took you hiking across the Grand Canyon how long did it take?" Lance sat his tray down and said, "It was a 24-mile hike it took four days, cost just over a thousand dollars, did you know there are pink rattlesnakes down there, and no dear old Dad did not take me, it was for school so I planned it booked it, and the Government put agent 444 with me to make sure I was safe, you worked with him in the Congo."

Patty Googled and said, "Hey you're right; there are pink rattlesnakes there did you see any." Lance said, "Sadly no, I did look at night, there are a lot of scorpions, I collected all three species the most dangerous was the Centruroides Exilicauda also known as the Bark scorpion, you catch them at night with a black light, they glow I had a light that was 450 nanometers that just light up the canyon floor." Patty asked, "And Rainer." Lance said, "Rainer took three days the first day was watching a film and doing basic instructions, let's see the Mountain is actually a massive stratovolcano, it is 14,410 feet high that is the highest mountain I have climbed and probably the last, been there done that."

Patty said, "Why is that, did you make the summit and why don't we leave the luggage in our room?" Lance smiled and said, "Yes I made the summit, everything went well but what did I gain doing that, I have more important things to do then climb a stupid mountain and I hate the cold, and about the luggage well I have a feeling we are going to be flying out of Ocho Rios, Dad isn't here, I am pretty sure of that, it would be great if he was but I think he is on that submarine."

Patty said, "You know Hilton always has a nice breakfast." Lance said, "And this is an all-inclusive resort, I explored the whole island last time I was here, I had security with me at all times that can be a drag sometimes." They finished breakfast and got into the Jeep it was a bluebird day not a cloud in the sky. Lance said, "Ok it says Ocho Rios is a little more than an hour and a half, our destination is just under an hour, almost to the Green Grotto Caves, have you ever been there?" She said, "No in fact this is the first time I have been to Jamaica." Lance said, "Well I recommend it, the tour is very nice, beautiful caves, they tell you the history and the science of the caves, this island survives on tourism."

Patty said, "It is a very clean place the beaches are beautiful." Lance said, "It is recommended that you stay on the hotels property at night, they want you safe, I didn't do any of the night life I think I was twelve." Alex spoke from Lance's pocket, "Slow down, do you see the mansion on the hill, I think that is where the live stream was sent, you will come to train tracks that cross the road and out to a pier." Lance slowed down and said, "It looks like we have armed guards, is there a way we could get an extraction team here?"

Alex said, "I am working this close to the chest, I don't know who to trust, I mean Specter is a web it has crawled into every part of the armed services, just go in there and if you don't come out in an hour, I will dig up somebody to get you out." Lance said, "How about a boat? We have the pier, there is no way we can outrun anyone with this Jeep." Alex said, "One boat coming up, be safe, and take care of the girl."

Alex turned off the Jeep and coasted to a stop just past the driveway. Patty got out the guard walked up. Lance said, "It just died; I might be out of gas." The man said, "I don't care you can't park here." Lance shrugged his shoulders and Patty shot him in the neck with a dart and he yelled in surprise and put his hand on his neck as his feet gave out and he crumbled to the ground. Lance said, "Quick let's get him in the ditch, how long will he be out?" Patty said, "They say an hour, but he is in pretty good shape so I say a half an hour." Lance asked, "Alex is there anymore."

Alex said, "Not that I see, and it is getting too hot for infrared, so be careful." Lance said, "We are going radio silent, whatever they took out of here was tall, and wide, you can see broken branches it has to be the laser." Lance walked down the driveway like he owned the place. Patty asked, "What are you doing." Lance said, "My Jeep broke down and I am looking for help, is this your first mission? If you look suspicious you will be." Patty said, "There the door, and a camera pointing at it."

Lance said, "Alex is there a way you can cut the power over here for a couple of minutes?" Alex said, "Working on it, you do know they are going to have backup generators." Lance said, "Yes sir, I hope this works, it is a keypad." Alex said, "You have a black out in three two one go." Lance held a button on his phone as he ran to the door and slammed the phone against the keypad. Patty was right behind him and said, "The power is back on." Lance said, "I am jamming the camera, come on."

The door slid open, they got in and he held the close button, he said, "Remember you have a license to kill," he could hear the sound of boots running their way. A man said, "Put your hands up." Lance said, "Didn't they tell you I was coming, you stupid oaf, I am here to check the doctor's calculations." Lance paced right in front of him he watched him taking his eyes off Patty who shot him in the neck, he said, "Christ," as he went to the floor. Lance said, "Let's do this quickly; find a computer," they went down the tunnel where it opened into a huge laboratory.

A man pulled out his pistol and said, "Stop right there." A man that seemed in charge said, "No guns keep it quiet." The man pulled a sword off the wall and said, "Ok boy, get over here." Lance smiled and said, "There has to be some mis-understanding," he walked up to the man jumped up to him did a throat chop, kicked him in the knee, and took the sword, and stuck him in the heart."

Patty kicked a guy right in the balls, did a round house kick taking him right off his feet. Another guy was running towards her from her back. Lance came around and took his head right off with the sword, blood shot out covering the floor. Patty said, "Quick get what you need and let's get out of here." A man took the other sword off the wall, and said, "I always wanted to do this, on guard boy." Lance took a stance, the man rushed him, Lance reached over with his right hand and grabbed onto his watch and shot two probes into the man from his watch, the man just shook from the stun.

Lance stepped in close and swung the sword and the man's head rolled right off his shoulders, he then ran to a bank of computers and someone yelled, "Lance over here." Lance looked and there was Mark in a cage. Lance said, "Grab a gun and get him out of there," he looked at the computers and tried to open one of them then he took out his phone and took a picture of something wrote on the wall next to the monitor. He heard Patty hammering on a lock on the cage Mark was held in. He said, "Quiet," and he ran over there.

He looked at her and said, "It's just a combination sliding barrel lock, don't they teach you anything?" He grabbed onto it and it came right apart. He looked at Mark and said, "Are you ok?" Mark said, "I slid down a chute and fell like ten feet into this cage, the floor dropped out from under me." Lance looked up and pulled out his phone zoomed it in and took a picture of the hinge that held the trap door. Patty took Mark's hand and helped him out of the cage and handed him a gun. Lance asked, "Do you have an escape plan?" Mark said, "On top of the hill I do not down here." Lance said, "Keep up old man, and watch the blood it could be slippery."

They got to the door and lance said, "Ok this is an all-out run to the Jeep and I hope to God we have a boat waiting for us." The door opened and they all started to run, Lance had his phone in his hand and was leading and sending messages as he ran. He could see a couple of cars came flying down the driveway of the mansion on top of the hill. Patty yelled, "Here they come." Lance hopped into the Jeep and had it running, as soon as Patty and Mark got there, he slammed it into reverse and then turned it down the tracks to the pier, and he was pushing forty by the time he was at the end. A cigar boat about a 28-footer pulled up.

Lance grabbed the luggage from the Jeep and threw it into the boat, while Patty and Mark got in; Lance jumped off the pier onto the deck and yelled "Go." By the time the cars pulled onto the pier they were gone. The driver said, "Yeah mon, you have the cash for this." Lance said, "Just get us out of here, head for Ocho Rios, how much were you promised?" The captain said, "A thousand dollars

American." Mark reached into his pocket and pulled ten hundred dollar bills off his money clip. Lance said, "Ok this is interesting, we have a little time to kill, shall we play tourists?"

The captain said, "Now we are passing Dunn River Falls, have you been there yet?" Mark said, "Isn't that the river you walk up?" Lance said, "It is covered with calcium carbonate, you have to wear those rubber shoes." Mark said, "Yeah that's right, boy that was a while ago, they said, you might get wet, I ended up swimming in it." Lance looked at his phone and asked, "Can we get off at this dock? We have a taxi waiting for us."

They pulled up to the dock, as Mark and Patty got off Lance gave the captain a couple of hundred and said, "You should disappear for a while and don't mention this fare to anyone," he threw the luggage onto the dock, and climbed up. Mark was standing by a taxi waving them over. Lance took his briefcase and luggage and Patty had hers, he asked, "How would you like to go on a cruise?" She said, "We have to find your father; the whole world is counting on us." They got in the driver asked, "Where to?"

Lance said, "The Carnival Conquest, did you know Rose is on this ship with Brent, we can wine and dine." Mark said, we don't have tickets, you just can't get on one of those things." They drove through the city the driver was telling them about some of the landmarks and things to do, he pulled up and Mark paid him. Mark said as soon as they started to walk, "As I said, you know people just can't hop aboard one of these things."

Lance said, "Alex, can we have someone meet us on the gangplank, to greet us aboard." Alex said, "What, wait, ok, sure there you are, the logistics of this is crazy, and that hinge is my patent, working on it." Lance said, "I have people, this sucks. At least Mark has a tux for the formal dinner, I always liked that about Carnival, people act different when they are dressed." Patty said, "This is amazing, I almost got killed today, and you guys act like it is nothing."

Lance said, "It is something, now we have to ask Mark how did you end up in that cage?" Mark said, "Well I went to this party at the mansion on the hill, agent 435 was there I followed her down the hall, she slammed the door in my face and someone shut the one behind me and the floor gave out, I slid down a chute a bet you a hundred feet and dropped into the cage, I thought I broke both my legs for a while, what is weird is nobody even talked with me." Patty said, "That is strange, don't you think?"

Lance said, "I don't think so, they knew he was coming, the agency has so many holes in it now, agents are disappearing, you probably would have been shark bait." They got to the ship, Mark said, "This isn't going to work." Lance had a huge smile and said, "Have faith," he walked up and said, "I am Henry Rose, this is Joyce Holdor, and the one who made us miss the cruise is my stepfather Mark Neal, we are catching up to our cruise, we missed the boat in New Orleans." The man said, "Yes your travel agent has contacted us several times, you do have photo identification right?"

Lance smiled and said, "Yes." He pulled out his passport looked the guy in the eye and said, "I am sorry for this, dad drinks a bit, not a way to start a vacation, I still have a balcony right." They went aboard and the luggage was searched, their photos were taken and they received a badge to wear. Lance asked, "Alex are you there?" His phone turned on and Alex came on with him saying, "I am busy you know."

Lance asked, "Is Mark the size of Brent? He needs clothes." Alex said, "Tell him to buy some, it's not like they don't have stores on the ship, show me the girl." Lance flipped the camera and pointed it toward Patty she said, "Hi Alex, hey you're dressed, did you get some sleep?" Alex said, "The whole world is in panic mode, there are armies under control of Spector, this satellite killer is just the tip of the iceberg, and by the way Mark looks like hell." Lance said, "He has had a long day, have you traced the hinge?" Alex said, "No, the hinge you really think that has something to do with it." Lance said, "It is just something that is out of the ordinary."

Patty said, "This is one big ship." Lance said, "It is a big one, it is 110,000 gross tons, 3000 passengers and over a thousand crew." They stepped into the lobby it was huge; Mark said, "I am getting a drink." Lance said, "be quick about it, I am starving." Patty asked, "Is your sister on the ship?" Lance said, "Yeah isn't that weird?" Mark walked up with a layered drink, he said, "This is a Superstar, a fruity vodka drink."

Lance said, "Go to your room and get freshened up give me a call in an hour." Mark took a long pull from his straw and said, "Sounds great," he headed to the shops to buy some clothes. Lance said, "Shall we check out our cabin? We are headed to the Empress deck, mid ship that is deck 7." Patty said, "This is nice, I wonder how many miles per gallon this thing gets."

Lance said, "I talked to a Captain once on a 7-day cruise they burnt thirteen hundred tons of fuel." Patty said, "Whoa that's a lot of fuel." She asked, "How many cruises have you been on?" Lance said, as they walked down the hall, "Seven, four Caribbean, one Mediterranean, one Alaskan, and one down the Mississippi." Patty said, "Your dad took you on some nice vacations."

Lance chuckled as he said, "No, no, he went on a Disney cruise in the Caribbean, that was a good time, I highly recommend it. Disney really knows how to treat you, if I could write a paper on it for school, he could write it off, so I have traveled the world, been to Antarctica for a month, boy that was a long flight, on the way there I stayed in Australia for a month, that was my early spring break." Patty said, "You went to the South Pole for spring break, I went to South Padre Island, Cancun, Punta Cana." Lance said, "I traveled the world one year and wrote a paper on Climate Change, pulled ice cores, studied the ground under the ice, you do know life on Earth the way we know it is done, the poles are melting which is raising the ocean levels and the salt water is getting diluted soon all the coral will die, and the Ocean fish, will have to adapt or die."

Patty said, "My God this ship is huge." Lance said, "There is a jogging track on the 13th floor I think, let see there are 1487 staterooms, 13 passenger decks, 22 bars and lounges, 4 swimming pools, and 18 elevators, yeah and it's not the biggest ship, that would be the Symphony of the Sea, a Royal Caribbean, it is 228,000-ton ship twice the size of this one, it holds 6680 passengers." Patty asked, "How do you remember all this?" Lance said, "Photograph memory, that is what makes school so easy."

They got to their room she said, "There is only one bed, you had better behave." Lance said, "I saved your life today, but I have a lot on my mind and sex is not one of them, food is though, let me take a quick shower and we can get a bite to eat, I love the buffets on these things." He sat his suitcase on the luggage rack and pulled out his laptop and plugged it in and said, "Alex." He turned his phone turned on and Alex said, "Now what?" Lance said, "I don't have internet."

Alex said, "Oh for Christ sakes, I have four generals online and just finished a video conference with the President, this runs deep." Patty said, over Lance's shoulder and said, "You had better lay off those energy drinks." Alex said, "Oh show me the girl." Lance flipped the camera and slowly scanned her from the feet to her face. Alex said, "That is damn nice, you have a job to do don't screw it up, the package is on its way and will be waiting for you, President Juan Garcia will be watching." Lance said, "Really are you going to be locked down again." Alex said, "I am free right now, all charges have been dropped, still don't know what they did with my parents, but they are safe." Lance said, "Thanks for the internet, and it's high speed." Patty said, after Lance ended the call, "He looks wound tight."

Lance said, "It looks like he is running the show, he gets like this but he gets stuff done," he winched as he took off his shirt. Patty said, "Shower and I will put more cream on those scabs, the burns look ok but the whip marks are inflamed." Lance said, "They are a bit tight." He quickly showered and came out in a towel. Patty said, "Lay down on the bed, and I will put this cream on." Lance said, "We don't have time for this, let me sit on the chair," he grabbed his laptop and sat down bending over so Patty could spread the cream on his back, he started to open file after file she asked, "What are you doing?"

Lance said, "I have AI running at the house, I have the same stuff Alex has we share a system, you just can't pull to much data or it will throw a flag, they gave Alex the green light." Lance's phone light and Alex said, "Now what do you want?" Lance said, "Sorry I mentioned your name, is that the United Nations behind you?" Alex said, "You have a job to do don't mess it up." Patty said, "Well I am taking a shower; you want to join?" Lance said, "Do a quick one, I have work to do, we have to meet Mark, and I am starving." She said, "Ok then," she slowly bent over and untied her shoes.

Lance stared for a second and said, "Really?" He opened another page on the laptop and said, "I can't work like this, would you hurry up." Patty went in the bathroom and was out in fifteen minutes. Lance said, "We are going for a snack, I have changed things around a bit tonight we have a sit-down meal with my sister in the main dining room." She said, "How did you do that?" Lance smiled and said, "It's all computerized, I just moved the people that were sitting at their table it will be a surprise." Patty asked, "Can I wear my bikini top?" Lance said, "You know you are beautiful, to get a snack yes but dinner no, we have to dress for that."

Mark called and said, "We are remaining on radio silence, I don't trust the agency one bit, the more I think of it, the more leaks I see, remind Patty not to check in, I will meet you up on the Lido deck." Lance looked over at Patty and said, "Mark said, not to check in, they will be monitoring your calls, they can't track you because that is not a company phone, now remember you are Joyce Holder."

She said, "Yes I am Joy asshole, I should file a complaint." Lance asked, "I still don't understand how people can wear flip flops." They got up to deck nine the Lido deck Lance called Mark, to find out where he was, then went through the buffet he said, "Joyce, we are eating in two hours so just get a snack." She smiled and said, "Yes Henry, whatever you say Henry." Lance sat at the table he had two plates one with a slice of lemon meringue pie, a brownie, the other a burger, fries, a pile of sliced ham, a slice of watermelon. He looked at Mark and asked, "You're done eating?"

He said, "No I got your text, we are having a proper sit down in two hours, I am just having some bread pudding and ice cream, remember I am old I don't have the metabolism of a 16-year-old." Patty sat down, Mark nodded and said, "Thank you again Joyce." Lance said, "You're having a salad, there is so much good food up there." Patty said, "That is one hell of a nice salad bar." Mark said,

"Those account numbers we found, they are cracking this case wide open, who is paying and who is getting paid." Lance said, "We are filling jails, but they still haven't found out who the big cheese is, I still think it is Vanbuick."

Mark said, "What, that family has been around for centuries I have been to parties at their house, they are too much of celebrities." Lance smiled and said, "Sometimes it is right in front of your face and you don't see it." Patty said, "I think it is the Russian Mob they just expanded." Mark said, "I will put a thousand dollars down on the Italians, they have been doing this for a hundreds of years, but why are they coming out into the light." Lance said, "The American mob was formed in 1869, with the Italians coming to New York, it is still running today, they have something up their sleeve, you are right why would they take such a chance, their forcing our hand." Patty said, "That's it, they have such a strangle hold on the armies, and the government they are looking at World Domination."

Lance shook his head and said, "Nobody is that stupid, many have tried and everyone has failed." Mark said, "Some people don't learn, and it has been a long time since some has tried." Lance said, with a half brownie in his hand, "The British were the closest to World Domination, then I think it was the Mongols under Genghis Khan, the Russians, the Germans." Patty said, "Don't forget the Americans; we have influence throughout the world."

Mark said, "But we are not stupid enough to try to run it." Lance said, "But we do have our noses in everyone's business, if you look at it the only wars, we needed to be in was the two World Wars, Vietnam, Korea, Iraq, Afghanistan, we have been at war 222 years out of the 239 years of existence, now that is a sad fact." Mark asked, "Is that right, it just doesn't sound right?" Patty sat her phone down and said, "You are just full of facts aren't you, Google says he is right."

Mark said, "Well I am off to the casino for an hour, and then I shall meet you at the main dining room." Lance said, "It's the Renoir located on decks three and four, it's a two-story dining room, table 465." Mark said, "I saved your text, see you there." Patty said, "We are going to an ice carving, catch a few rays on the deck." Lance said, "Fine by me."

At 5:30 Lance and Patty showed up at the table, Lance had a shirt and tie, and Patty was wearing a short floral dress. The waiter walked by and asked, "Are you at the right table?" Lance said, "Henry Rose, Joyce Holdor, Mark Neal, Julia Robinson, and Brent Logan, I shuffled some people around, all is good, and the two other couples were paid off." He held up a hundred-dollar bill, and said, "For your inconvenience."

The man looked at his i-pad smiled and reached down took the bill and said, "Everything is well, would you like a beverage?" Lance said, "Mark hold up your card, we will have a fine Monet Champagne." Patty said, "How about a Dom Perignon if he is buying?" Mark asked, "What year of Bollinger do you have?" The server said, "Sorry sir the top-of-the-line champagne is a fine bottle of Epernay Dom Perignon Brut." Mark said, "Fine we will have that, and have another close by." Lance said, "Thank you, we did save your life." Mark asked, "How long am I going to be paying for that?"

Lance said, "You charge everything to the job and what you don't you write off, would you like to know how much you have in stocks and bonds and your three offshore accounts?" Mark stared at him for almost a minute without saying a word, then he said, "How?" Lance smiled and said, "I have a guy, you were left a large inheritance, which is fine but you killed the guy what was it 250 million." Mark smiled and said, "I am good but not cheap, and we don't air our laundry in the public."

Brent came to the table, and asked, "How did you guys get here?" Mark stood held out his hand to Rose took it and he knelt kissing the back of it saying, "Miss Julia so happy to see you." She blushed and said, "How did you get on the ship; it must have been Alex he has been following us." Lance's phone dinged, he answered it and said, "Sorry it was Julia she said your name." Alex said, "Well let me see her." Lance flipped the camera and showed Rose is a light-yellow sundress he said, "Very nice the yellow, with the dark hair, and beautiful brown eyes, are you enjoying the cruise."

Rose said, "Oh yes thank you so very much, I am enjoying myself," she stepped up to Bent and kissed him lightly on the lips." Mark looked a little depressed. Lance said, "Now don't be getting too attached to him, you don't need another heart break." Julia said, "We are a couple, enjoying life." The waiter took their order he asked, Lance. Mark said, "Watch this." Lance said, "Ok shall we start out with Strawberry Bisque, fried Calamari, then Alligator tail, Veal Parmesan, the Surf and Turf, that is Lobster and Filet Mignon, and for dessert I will have the Melting Chocolate cake." Patty said, "And don't worry he will eat it all." Rose asked, "Are you and Lance a thing?"

Patty smiled and said, "Everything is going well; don't worry I am taking good care of your brother." Rose looked at Lance and said, "All work and no play makes Lance a boring boy." Lance said, "This is about Dad, don't worry about me sis." Rose looked at Patty and said, "I am sorry he is one of a kind, but he is my little brother." Patty smiled and said, "I am playing his nurse; everything is healing well." Lance squeezed her leg under the table; she looked at him and mouthed, "Sorry."

Rose asked, "What is going on?" Mark said, "I found your brother chained and was being tortured to keep your father working." Rose looked shocked and asked, "Are you alright, you still haven't found him?" Lance smiled and said, as he looked at Mark, "Everything is fine now; all we have to do is to find him, and we have a lead." The food came and Patty was right Lance finished before anyone. They made plans to meet later, Mark said, "I am going for a drink, then I will watch the news and get a good night sleep." Lance pointed at his watch; Mark nodded slightly.

Lance and Patty went and freshened up and met Mark at the cigar lounge for five minutes, when they got out Patty said, "I love the smell of a good cigar, but you smell like it for the rest of the night." Lance said, "I never got into smoking, there is no logical reason to do that to your body, now drinking is a different story, if you watch what you are doing and don't overindulge it is fine."

Patty said, "You have been to how many colleges." Lance smiled and said, "I learned how to drink in Mad Town, I can drink a case of beer a day, you just have to pace yourself." Patty said, "Ok we meet your sister at the Disco, do you think her and Brent. . .?" Lance said, "Stop right there, they are just having a good time, she uses men like toilet paper, and she uses them and throws them away." Patty said, "That is how she became a headliner." Lance said, "Sure why not?" Patty said, "A lot of women have slept their way to the top."

Lance reached out for her and hugged her and asked, "Are you that type of woman? We have to put on a show for Rose so she thinks we are doing the nasty, or she will bug us all night, for a while she thought I was gay." Patty said, "Really, so you two aren't that close? Lance said, "We were just into different things, Mom left, and I was more like Dad and she always was looking for attention, dragged me to all her plays, and drama, my God she was going to marry a professor once." Patty asked, "She thought you were gay." Lance said, "I have played on both sides of the fence. I am not looking for a relationship right now."

They went into the Disco and found Brent and Rose. Patty pulled Lance out on the dance floor Lance struck a pose then started to dance like John Travolta in Grease. He reached out and pulled her into Tango and danced up to the table. Brent said, "You have some moves." Rose said, "He isn't bad, we won a few dance contests." Lance said, "I had a hell of a time lifting her." Brent said, "Really? That is hard to believe."

Rose said, "He was seven and I was twelve, we did well together, Dad made him do it." Lance said, "What a waste of time, all that practicing touring around the nation going to all the contests." Rose said, "That was the best time of my childhood." Lance said, "I had to come home from college to dance with her." Mark said, "So you are like six years younger, and you went from high school to college and was singing and dancing?" Lance said, "She left high school and went straight to Vegas, almost killed the old man." Rose said, "But I made it, I am headlining my own show, come on let's dance." Lance said, "I am a little stiff; I just had a sword fight." Rose giggled and said, "This kid, was sent to Japan to learn to control his anger, I think it was Tai Chi, he picked up sword fighting and then he did fencing, everything this guy tried, he aced."

Lance rolled his eyes and went out on the floor and you could tell they were professional Dancers everyone stopped to watch, they discoed, then the Charleston, the Fox Trot, Tango, Quickstep, the Cha Cha Cha, Rumba, Rose held up her hands, and they walked off to a round of applause. Lance pulled her into a hug and said, "You are getting out of shape." Rose said, "And you are stiffing up old man." Lance smiled and said, "It has been a long three weeks, let's go to the piano bar and have a night cap, I am tired."

They went back to the table and Lance said, "Drink up we are going to the piano bar then it is bed for me, it has been a long day." Mark raised his glass and said, "To a successful mission." Lance said, "I thought you were going to watch the news and go to bed?" Mark smiled and said, "I am doing it." Everyone raised their glass and took a drink; Lance stared out into space Patty asked, "Are you ok." Lance said, "Oh yes, it has just been a really long day, the time is winding down, the window of opportunity is shrinking."

Patty asked, "Are they going to pay the trillion dollars?" Rose said, "A trillion for Dad that's a bit steep." Brent said, "No it is a trillion to stop them from shooting down three satellites." Mark said, "They are going to do it anyway; you know that and I know that." Lance said, "No they won't, we just have to save the old man, shall we go and have a nightcap at the piano bar, and call it a night." Mark said, "I will see guys in the morning." Lance said, "Cozumel here we come." Patty slid her around Lance as they walked down the hall and asked, "What is in Cozumel." Lance smiled and asked, "You haven't been there have you, well Cozumel was created by a large asteroid they figure around six miles in diameter, hit leaving a hole 122 miles wide, that was around 66 million years ago. It was discovered back in 1518 by Juan de Grijalva, there were over three thousand Mayans living there. Now in 1570 Cortez and his men went in and looted the place destroying a lot of temples, and they brought smallpox there by the 1600s the island was completely abandon."

Patty asked, "What does Cozumel mean, is it the people that lived there?" Lance gave her a little hug and looked into her eyes and said, "No that's not it, it means island of swallows, you should take the Tulum Mayan tour, I have never been on it but it looks nice I went to Chichen Itza for a class field trip, I took a class in Anthropology, that was interesting." Patty asked, Rose "What hasn't this kid done?" Rose smiled and said, "He isn't a real medical doctor, he does have a few doctorates, let's see he has only had one real relationship, she broke his heart."

Lance said, "Don't listen to her; she goes through guys like they are going out of style." Rose said, "How would you know; you see me like three times a year." Lance said, "I catch your show every two weeks, and I do say you are so much better then when you started." They went into the piano bar and found a table. Lance said, "A half an hour and then I am going to bed." The show was between a comedy act and a musical one, the guy was good, Rose asked him if Lance could play.

The guy smiled and said, "Sure sit right down and we can see what you can do." Lance looked at Rose with contempt, and asked, "Why would you do that?" Rose said, "Oh Joyce would like to hear you play." Lance got up and sat at the piano he looked at Rose and mouthed, "I hate you," he put his hands on the keys and said to the piano man, "I haven't touched the keys in months, this is Moonlight Sonata by Bach." He started to play and just played the song perfectly, when he was done, he received a standing ovation. The piano man said, "That was perfect, you nailed it."

Lance's eyes rolled up to meet Patty's, he blew her a kiss. He got up and said to Patty, "It is getting late, I need a good night sleep tomorrow is going to be a long day." Rose said, "I told you he could play, and he has always been a party pooper." Lance said, "No I use my time wisely, tomorrow is going to be a busy day, and you should get some sleep. Are you going diving tomorrow the water is so clear in Cozumel." Rose said, "We haven't decided yet, I was thinking of horse riding." Patty said, "On these touristy places you usually get old nags, what do you think Lance." Lance said, "Good night, I have to get some sleep, you can stay up if you want to." She smiled and said, "No I think you are right good night; we will see you in the morning." Rose said, "You two go right to sleep now." Lance shook his head and said, "Don't stay up to long, and always stay sharp." Bent said, "Don't worry. I have everything under control."

As Lance and Patty walked down the hall, he said, "That guy just doesn't get it, Specter is going to be on the lookout for her, and they used me to keep Dad working." Patty said, "Tomorrow is the day they shoot down the satellites." Lance said, "We can discuss this in our room." They walked for another ten minutes and Patty said, "My God this is a big ship." Lance said, "There are 3,000 passengers sleeping, and the ship is 953 feet long, and she has a beam of 116 feet."

Lance opened the room, stepped inside and said, "Ok, you might think you are safe talking about Specter, their people go on vacation too." Patty gave him a hug, Lance kissed her neck passionately up to her ear, slid one hand down and cupped her butt, and whispered, "You are such a beautiful girl." She pushed him away and said, "Let me freshen up." She went to the bathroom, Lance undressed folded everything and put it in his suitcase and laid out what he was going to wear the next day on top of it and moved it close to the door. Patty stepped out of the bathroom wearing lingerie. Lance cooed "Oh very nice, that is Victoria Secret, a wicked cutout teddy." She smiled and said, "You know your lingerie."

Lance said, "I have even designed some this is made well and is comfortable," he ran his hands over the sides of it pulling her closer to he, their mouths met he pulled down her straps and started to kiss her shoulders, and he worked down from there, soon the teddy was laying on the floor. Patty said, "No, stop we shouldn't."

Lance said, "I saved your life, you like me don't you, and you want this as much as I do." He kissed her passionately, pulled away and looked into her eyes and said, "If you want to stop, we can right now." She stared into his eyes and pulled him into a long kiss running her hands down to guide in his manhood. Twenty minutes later Lance was in the bathroom setting out his disguise, with his briefcase on the counter. Patty stepped up behind him, giving him a hug her bare breasts on his back, she whispered in his ear, "So you are going to be Henry tomorrow," she slid her hands around him and kissed his neck.

Lance looked into the mirror to look her in the eyes and said, "That was wonderful, but we really have to get some sleep, it is going to be a long day tomorrow, and remember you are Joyce." She said, "Get out of here and let me pee, I will meet you in bed." Lance took the side of the bed that was closest to the door, Patty walked in and stood naked looking out the balcony sliding glass window. Lance said, "You do know you are beautiful." She turned and slipped into bed and cuddled up to him, and said, "You told me the definition of beautiful before," she ran her hand across his hip. Lance said, "Nope not going to happen, I need sleep," he kissed her lightly and rolled over.

Chapter Twelve: U-Boat

The ship docked early in the morning, Lance slipped out of bed and put on his disguise once again he was Henry Rose, he quietly stepped out of the cabin carrying his briefcase, and he went to the breakfast buffet. They were just setting up, the bartender was wiping down the bar, and Lance set his briefcase on a table and got himself a coffee and a few pastries. He sat down and pulled out his laptop.

Mark walked up with a cup of coffee, and asked, "What is the plan?" Lance turned the laptop to show him a red dot in the Pacific Ocean, he said, "The gang plank drops in twenty minutes, there will be a cab waiting for us, we are going to be cutting it real close," he got up and went to the bar then to the buffet, came back with a plate of hash and biscuits and gravy with bacon laying on top, he sat it on the table and went back to the bar and brought back two Bloody Mary's. Mark said, "This is 500 miles; we are not going to make it."

Lance said, with a mouth full "You had better eat something, were not stopping for a meal, gang plank drops in 15 minutes," he took the laptop and zoomed in on Cozumel. Mark got back from the buffet with a cherry turnover, he looked at the screen. Lance said, "You're going to have to eat it on the way, our cab just pulled up, let's go." Lance showed a shipmate his badge and said, "We won't be sailing back; we have a plane to catch." The guy scanned the badge, Mark held out his and got his scanned also.

Lance said, "Come on old man, we have to get in the air." They power walked down the pier, Mark said, "Great we are going to get sweaty before we even start the day." Lance said, "You are in Mexico what did you expect?" Mark said, "Nice Ocean breeze, sun, and sand." Lance jogged to the cab and showed the driver his phone and a fifty-dollar bill. Mark got there as soon as the door closed the cab was moving, ten minutes later they pulled over to a marina. Lance handed the driver another twenty. Mark said, "This is getting interesting, where are we going?" Lance said, "To save my dad, I hope." Lance started to jog down the pier, Mark was following then he yelled "That thing is an antique." Lance got to the seaplane and boarded and yelled, "Cast off the ropes." Mark untied the tail and the front, holding onto it. Lance fired the old plane up and started to run some RPMs, checking the flaps, and the rudder.

Mark pushed off and hopped aboard; he sat in the copilot's seat and asked, "Do you know how to fly this thing?" Lance pointed to his headset as he powered up the plane, turned it into the wind and took off. Mark said, "This is a Grumman G-73 Mallard; they stopped making these in 1951." Lance said, "We bought it at an online auction, it is a museum piece, they had the engines changed over to a turboprop, we had the wings x-rayed for cracks, and everything looks good." Mark asked, "What are we going to do if we find the submarine?"

Lance said, "Let's give it a minute and make sure the cruise control is working, close enough, come on back." Mark followed Lance to the back of the plane, there were two crates marked LP refrigerator. Lance said, "Here is a screw gun unassembled the crates, put the screws in the bucket, we have set up a couple of aid camps in the jungle, Red Cross uses this plane a lot, it is usually parked in the Amazon, Dr. Johanson runs a dozen jungle hospitals." Mark asked, "You let him use it for free?" Lance said, "Nothing is free, now give me a hand." Mark took hold of the top cover and lifted and said, "Missiles, where did you get missiles." Lance said, "This is what put Alex in house arrest."

Lance's phone went off it was Rammstein du hast, he said, "Alex I like the ring tone, we are in the air, now you are sure these are going to work." Alex said, "In theory, pull the strips in the warheads, are you over water?" Lance said, "No we are not." Alex said, "Oh I got you, yeah I would wait, I have been scanning for the U-boat but nothing yet." Lance asked, "And General Star?" Alex said, "He is on the way in an old C-130, he has details of the mission, with a handpicked crew." Lance said, "Keep looking for the sub, we still have three hours."

Alex said, "Keep quiet, there are a lot of people monitoring this, it is hard to tell the good guys from the bad, good luck, wrap you phone, oh yeah Garcia will be watching." Lance said, "That works, keep in touch." Mark asked, "So what was the red dot, and how does this work? You are going to shoot the sub and hope you don't kill your father?" Lance said, "This is an EMP an electromagnetic pulse, it will disable the sub, and the red dot is the coordinates."

Mark asked, "Why not use a railgun?" Lance said, "It's not the same, this is lighter, and will cover a large area, the right weapon for the right job." Mark asked, "So who is this Garcia you were talking about." Lance said, "He is a prospective buyer, the stinger missile is small and effective, we are ready to show it off it will be the first test of the weapon, our government just locked up my friend, the money is in the arms race." Mark asked, "You have never shot one off, what happens if it doesn't work."

Lance smiled and said, "It works on paper; we have double checked everything." Mark said, "I don't like this; I have worked with engineers before most of them have no common sense." Lance said, "We have one shot; this has to work." Mark said, "You have two missiles." Lance smiled and said, "Ok we have two shots; we have used AI to build them." Mark said, "Yeah I was just on a mission cleaning up a mess with AI." Lance said, "Doctor Morrow, in Colorado."

Mark said, "That is top secret, just a hand full of people knew about that." Mark said, "It was put into a computer, my friend has open reign, he is running several super computers, it's not Bob a smaller version, we call him Robbie he is using other countries hardware, by the way how did the robots move, could they run." Mark said, "Run, you couldn't tell them apart from people, the whole base was operated by them." Lance said, "Morrow he was an odd duck, it was creepy working there." Mark asked, "Did you help build the killer scorpions." Lance asked, "Were they poisonous?" Mark said, "They were huge, seven feet long huge pinchers, they would impregnate a host by stabbing it with its tail and shooting in an egg, the baby would eat its host." Lance said, "So that is what killed him, I just glanced at the report." Mark said, "That's not what did him in; it was Alexa, a woman AI left the door open on purpose, ok you're right he was eaten by a scorpion baby."

Lance said, "That's not a good way to go; I always thought a robot would have killed him because he gave it to many emotions." Mark said, "That was it, he pissed her off so she had him killed, and my God I have to find a different job, this is just getting so weird." Lance said, "I thought you were retired."

Alex turned on Lance's phone and said, "Five minutes cut the power, glide in and land on the back side of the island, it looks like deep water right up to the beach." Mark asked, "What are we doing?" Lance said, "We can't fire those missiles from their crates, we have to assemble them and strap them to the plane." Alex said, "In less than seventeen minutes, you are cutting this close." Lance said, "I take it you have spotted the U-Boat." Alex said, "That's a big ten four good buddy." Lance asked, "The Chinese jamming system is it operative."

Alex said, "It is out of range, and our killer satellites I have one arming now." Mark asked, as lance banked the plane into a corkscrew, "Killer satellites, don't they hunt other satellites." Lance said, "They have never been used, but theory has it you could shoot a man three thousand miles away." Mark said, "So they should be able to hit a submarine." Lance said, "Should be able to slice it in half." Mark smiled and said, "That should do it, but I would doubt they would have that much power." Lance said, "That's the last resort, neither one of these have been tried in the field."

Lance sat the plane down easy on the water and said, as he coasted up to the shore, "I hope he is right, if it is coral, we could rip the bottom of this thing open." Mark asked, "So what are we going to attach the missiles on with duct tape?" Lance said, "We don't have much time, each section weighs fifty-two pounds, you get out and I will hand them to you, and we will assemble them on the beach, there is a box of brackets that should fit the plane."

Mark got out and pulled the plane farther on the beach. Lance got the top off the crate and struggled to get the first section out of the packing, he sat it on the deck of the plane and slid it out the door, Mark took it and walked a few feet to set it on the beach. Lance said, as he handed Mark a box and said, these are the brackets, here comes the second missile keep them separate." Lance said, as he handed Mark the last section of the missile, "That took seven minutes, we have ten minutes to get back in the air."

Mark said, "That's cutting it close." Lance said, "Don't talk just listen, we need to pull out the insulator covering the battery, hold up the front I will unscrew the warhead, there we go, now hold it as I assemble the third stage, there color coded and they will only fit one way, let me get the brackets." Mark said, "This damn thing is heavy." Lance said, "It is just over two hundred pounds, let me pull out the insulator strips on theses, we have a green light, I will take the tail you take the nose and we will mount this thing." Lance stepped out into the ocean, they lifted the missile and Lance asked, "Can you hold this thing up by yourself as I get the brackets on?" Mark worked himself to the middle holding the missile above his head.

Lance snapped the bracket to the plane and guided the missile into it, then stepped around Mark and mounted that one." Lance said, "We have to make up time," he ran to the nose of the next one and started to unscrew the warhead pulling out the insulator, Mark brought the next piece and locked it in place and the third and then the tail. He said, "I got this; get the brackets ready," he carried the missile to the other side of the plane, Lance ran around him and locked the bracket on the wing and helped Mark lift the missile and locked it into place, then he fastened the front bracket and locked the missile to it. Mark grabbed onto the nose cone and shook it. Lance looked at him and asked, "What are you doing?"

Mark said, "Well you don't want them falling off." "Lance said, as he was looking at his phone and the brackets, getting them to blink green, "Check the other side." Mark walked around and shook the plane with the missile; he said, "They aren't going anywhere." Lance entered in the missile into his phone, and said, "Let's shove off."

The two men pushed the plane offshore, Lance got in and fired up the engines and Mark turned the plane and climbed on the pontoon as Lance was picking up speed. Lance turned to Mark and said, "That took twenty-two minutes five minutes more than we had, were going to have to burn some fuel," he put the throttle to the max, the airspeed started to climb as did the altimeter. Mark asked, "Where did you get those missiles? They cost over a half million apiece." Lance said, "Black market, eight hundred grand, and to build a weapons grade EMP is eighty grand, after all said, and done, we can do it for twenty now."

Mark said, "Electromagnetic pulse is nuclear; we are not going to get out of the way of the fall out." Lance turned and looked at him and said, "Do you think I am that stupid to fire off a nuclear bomb while we are in this Mallard the top speed is 215 miles per hour? We would be fried crispy." Mark asked, "So how does it work?" Lance said, "The missiles are charging now, they will build up to ten thousand volts, once we fire them it will go to a million, and turn into plasma, anything within a mile will be fried." Mark asked, "Do you mean knocked out for a few minutes or fried forever?"

Lance said, "Anything within five miles should be fried, we should be fine we will be knocked out for a minute or so, the ship should be dead in the water, the pulse should be large enough to fry the Resistors, Inductors, and the Transistors, sometimes the Capacitors depends what kind they are." Mark asked, "Is this on paper, or have you tried them?" Lance said, "Three tests, we are ready for a showing, I am turning controls to you, take it up to 15 thousand feet."

Mark asked, "Are you sure this thing will fly that high?" Lance said, "It will fly at 23,000 feet just do it." Mark pulled back the yoke and started to climb. Lance said, "There is our C-130 about thirty-five miles out." Lance said, "Give me your phone; hurry," He ran in back and grabbed a lead lined photo bag. Mark pulled out his phone and handed it to him. Lance made a call he said, "General, wrap your phone, the sub is in sight."

Lance fired off both sidewinder missiles; he said, "Shut off the plane, cut the power." Mark yelled "What?" Lance hit the power switch; the engines came to a stall. A red light shined a beam into the sky, one missile blew a green blast, and it shook the plane. The red light that was shooting into space went out, the second missile kept flying straight at the submarine and it hit the sub blowing off the tail. Mark turned and said, "Your dad is on there." Lance said, "It is a chance we had to take, now head for that ship."

Mark said, "Paratroopers." Lance said, "Yeah that could be interesting I hope they can get their plane started again, it was far enough away, I hope." Mark tried starting the Mallard and made it come alive, he banked it coming level with the water coming to the U-Boat fast, he said, "Those guys are going to have machine guns." Lance said, "I think you are right, let's get out of here, they are abandoning ship."

Mark said, "But you're Dad." Lance said, calmly "Alex, do you see Dad, they are taking to lifeboats, and the sub is going down." Alex said, "I am bringing on a spy satellite now, General do you copy." An old man's voice responded, "Yes I copy." Alex said, "The second boat has the prize; I repeat the second boat has the prize." The General said, "Roger." Lance asked, "Is he ok." Alex said, "How the hell am I supposed to know? There are fifteen people in that raft, the U-boat just rolled over maybe it won't sink."

Mark said, "Well we did stop the satellites from being shot down." Lance said, "It's a waiting game now." Mark asked, "Where to now?" Lance asked, "Alex are we clear for Acapulco, and are you watching the old man." Alex said, "Everything is a go, you are cleared, and the troops are on landing on the ship, and we have one on your dad's lifeboat, there are four Blackhawks on their way, in time we shall see if it has been a success." Lance said, "I can't thank you enough." Alex said, "Over and out."

Mark said, "Acapulco, that sounds like fun." Lance said, "We are there just for fuel, then to Cancun for the night and meet up with the girls in New Orleans." Mark said, "I am getting too old for this." Lance said, "This is just the start, there is a war brewing, Specter is everywhere." Mark said, "Maybe they will go back underground." Lance said, "We have enough evidence to infiltrate their ranks and find out who is behind it all."

They refueled at Acapulco and were back in the air in an hour, almost made it to Cancun when Lance's phone turned on. Alex said, "I have someone who wants to talk to you." Lance's dad Adam's face appeared on the phone, Lance said, "Hi Doc, glad to see I didn't kill you, sorry it took so long, and I see you got the laser to work." His Dad said, "I am so glad you are alright, and you were right the EMP worked, but how?"

Lance said, "Now that is top secret, we will talk when this is all done." Mark said, "Doctor Adam Johnson I presume, this is bigger than you think trust no one, and I do mean nobody is safe." Lance said, "He is right you know, glad to have you back, enjoy your debriefing." Adam said, "This is going to be a nasty one; I hope I don't land in jail." Lance said, "That's not going to happen; you thought it was a legit government program, hell I even worked on it, the system is broken, and we have to fix it."

Adam said, "I just don't understand, how can I work on a project for over a year and not know it is the enemy, I mean they paid well, we were even in army bases." Lance said, "A lot of people were fooled, I will see what kind of pull I can get, it is just so hard to tell the good guys from the bad, Senator Brady he is Specter, we have links that show he is dirty, this is not a secure line, we will strategize when this is over," he held the power button on the phone. Mark said, "This is a bad one; it could take years and evolve hundreds if not thousands of people." Lance said, "Worldwide domination, this time everything is in place, we have AI running down every phone call, and connecting them it is like a huge spiders web it grows with every call, ever person is getting investigated."

Mark asked, "So have you ever been to Cancun?" Lance said, "Spring break, then for a couple of months after we worked with the Underwater Museum, the electrical grid, the sewage system, I made some money but most of it was to upgrade their system, I wrote a paper on it and got a A- not my best work but everything runs smoothly now."

Mark asked, "You went to Cancun for spring break and worked?" Lance smiled and said, "When you go somewhere and see a problem, or a way you can make it better, you do it right?" Mark said, "No: you party, girls, drinks, sun, and sand, what is an underwater museum anyway?" Lance said, "Art underwater, hundreds of statues, and cars, and houses, it is like a manmade reef, it holds a lot of fish, you can rent a glass bottom boat, scuba dive, it's a tourist thing, but a lot of locals dive there." Mark asked, "What resort are we staying at?" Lance smiled and said, "Airport hotel, the Marriott we eat and right to bed, the ship gets to New Orleans and disembarks by 10:00."

Mark asked, "What are your plans after you have competed your mission?" Lance smiled and said, "That was just the tip of the iceberg, we have to unravel the whole thing to straighten it out, it could take years, and I really don't want to do this." Mark said, "Well I am back at square one; this didn't help me finding out who is behind it all." Lance said, "Give it time, Dad should have some insight of what is going on, and I am sure he has a grasp on the dealings of Specter." Lance looked at Mark and said, "Henry Rose can stay in the briefcase, I book the hotel under you, it's like a hundred bucks."

They got to the hotel and Lance showed his phone to the receptionist, and said, "We need keys to room 128." She looked up the room on the computer and asked, "Could I see the card that was used to book the room?" Lance looked at her and said, "Really, I don't think so." She said, "It is policy, and picture id." Lance said to Mark "She wants to see your Visa card." Mark gave him a strange look and pulled out his card and handed it to her with his driver's license. Lance flashed her his id, and said, "If I had more time I would drag your manager out here, everything was done right all I needed was the key cards."

Mark said, "You're a little harsh aren't you?" Lance looked up at him and said, "It has been a very long day, and I know what I am doing, I am not just a customer, I am a stockholder, and I hate when people screw with me, this transaction should have taken two minutes." Mark said, "Just chill, you are a little stressed." Lance said, "And starving and tired." Mark took the key cards and started for the elevators and said, "I wonder if the agency got my luggage from Jamaica." Lance said, "You can't be contacting your agency, it has been compromised, find someone you trust and we will check them out, this runs deep." Mark asked, "And why should I trust you." Lance said, "Let's hit the buffet then go to our room."

Lance walked into the dining room and put his briefcase on a table and the both of them went to the buffet, Mark said, "Take what looks fresh, I don't trust buffets you don't know how long the food has been sitting there." Lance smiled as he started to fill his plate, he had chicken, a hamburger, some jerked chicken, 3 different kinds of pork, beans, salsa, and he sat down with a heaping plate. Mark sat down with a small salad and some fruit cheese and crackers; he said, "If I ate like that, I would be three hundred pounds."

Lance smiled and pulled a large shrimp off his plate peeled it and dipped it in salsa, he said, "Did you see the dessert table?" Mark smiled as he slowly ate, watching Lance devour his plate. Lance looked up and asked, "How long do you think they will have Dad in custody." Mark said, "I would think a month, this is a big deal, if he doesn't play his cards right, he could go to prison for a very long time."

Lance said, "Ok one lap around the dessert table and we will be out of here." Mark said, "Grab me one of those chocolate sponge cake things." Lance filled his plate with deserts, and sat down with two plates, he slid one in front of Mark and said, "Your sponge cake with hot chocolate dipping sauce looks yummy." Mark said, "You're going to eat all of that before you go to bed?" Lance said, "Not a problem, I will brush my teeth, it's amazing the work they put into these, and one bite they are gone." Mark said, "They do a lot with bananas." Lance said, "The chocolate covered strawberries are delicious, they are perfectly ripe, and the dark chocolate is good too."

Mark said, "You do know your sister is going to have to go into witness protection, she will have to give up her career." Lance looked up and said, "That is not going to happen, we will give her some security, but she is living her dream right now, you don't know the strings we had to pull to get her the job." Mark said, "She is good." Lance said, "She is good but not great, she is headlining an act, the longer she is on the sidelines the better her chances her understudy gets the part." Mark asked, "So what is the game plan?" Lance said, "Up at five, in the air by six, in New Orleans by ten, meet up with the girls by eleven."

Mark said, "That is not what I mean, you got your dad, are you going to step back into your old life." Lance said, "Dad has his work I have mine, it works this way, he is going to be gone for a while, I will tie up all the loose ends, I have some dealing with the EMP that worked just as it was planned." Mark said, "Sell it to the highest bidder." Lance said, "Kind of. Uncle Sam always puts up a nice bid, then they will use it or bury it, happens more than you think."

They walked into their room Lance said, "Remember radio silence, no contacting anyone." Mark said, "How about you, you're contacting your friend?" Lance smiled and said, "You try to hack our program and see what happens, it is vicious we can track down the user and fry its system, or plant a worm, wipe out their bank account, two years ago an antivirus company sent out a deadly virus, we tracked it down the guy is spending twenty years for that and we dissolved their company because it went right to the top management, boy did we make money off of that one." Mark asked, "So it is business as usual?"

Lance said, "No it will never be the same, change is inevitable the whole world has changed because of this we are going to be on the hunt forever, Specter is running some countries, it is high in the food chain, look at the armed services, and the government, we don't know who to trust, is money being siphoned off to this mob." Mark said, "You call it a mob."

Lance took off his shoes and said, "What else would you call it? Specter is organized crime, in a global size, we just have to find the link, North America is linked with South, but that is where it stops, we have ran Asia but it doesn't link with Africa, we have the finest computers running at max speed, they are compiling all the information, AI works very well, that is going to be our next big war." Mark said, "I am showering in the morning," he stripped down and crawled into bed. Lance showered, shaved, and hit the hay. The morning came and Mark was showered and ready to start the day by the time Lance woke up. Lance looked at his phone and said, "The plane is ready and the flight plan is booked."

Chapter Thirteen: New Orleans, Find the Girls

They got to the airport the plane was fueled and ready to go, it was a bright and sunny day. Mark said, "This is one of those days regular retired guys have a couple of beers play a round of golf and just enjoy the day." Lance said, "Why don't you take a walk around the old girl make sure nothing is falling off? It is an antique after all." Mark chuckled and said, "You do know I was praying this thing was going to start after that EMP." A huge smile formed on Lance's face as he said, "So was I, did I tell you the C130 dropped over 10,000 feet before they got the engines to start, the General must have shit a brick." Mark walked around the plane, checking the wings and the landing gear; he was knocking on the pontoons when Lance stepped up.

Mark asked, "Do you have a Crescent wrench, we are carrying a few hundred pounds of water, it looks like there are a few rivets that are loose, must have hit a rock." Lance walked over to the cargo bay and took out a toolbox and handed him a wrench and said, "A 12-inch adjustable wrench, Crescent is a brand name." Mark unscrewed the plug and water streamed out. After a minute lance said, "Wow that is a lot of water, so how long am I going to be stuck with agent Patty? She is nice but I do not need a babysitter." Mark said, "She is cute, enjoy the company, go on a vacation, I like the way she blushes when you call her Joy-ass." Lance said, "I do enjoy her company, but there is work to do."

Mark screwed the plug back in the pontoon, and said, "We should get better gas mileage now, there are a few loose rivets, other than that she is a fine-looking plane." Lance said, as he climbed the stairs "There are only a few dozen left in the world, one day we will sell her, right now it is a write off, it is used in my South American charity." Mark sat in the copilot's seat and asked, "You have a charity." Lance smiled and said, "Yes, I have three, you should look into that, why give the government all the money when you can put it to good use, I have a 40,000-acre ranch, the Boy Scouts use it, six other nonprofit use it, and I wrote the whole thing off, the taxes every year are taken off, the rich don't pay taxes they pay lawyers." Mark said, "So you are rich?" Lance said, "I am well off not rich, now you are rich, you have what 265 million."

Mark said, "Whoa there, and how do you know that? Before you said, I had 280 some million." Lance fired up the engine and said, AI, every stop light you have been through in the last three years we know, every time you walked into a bank, we know, every hotel, every credit card transaction, we know except Niihau that is a safe zone." Mark said, "So you can't see what happens on Hawaii?" Lance said, "I did not say that, just Niihau, and we can but chose not to, the security is tight on the island, and it might not look it." Mark said, "I have been through the server, you have 360-degree coverage."

Lance said, "We have clearance to take off;" he rolled onto the runway and took off toward New Orleans." Mark said, "You do know it would have been faster to fly commercial, it is only like six hundred miles." Lance said, "It is six hundred and thirty-seven, and there are no direct flights, you either go to South Carolina, or to Texas, so this is the quickest, it will take around three hours." Mark smiled and said, "So I didn't research it." Lance asked, "Are you done with this mission or are you going to find out who is behind this and kill them?" Mark said, "Whoa, kill them is that what you think we do?"

Lance said, "I have seen your resume, I know everything that is in your record, and I know Pierce we use his place to park and excess our server." Mark said, shocked, "That is yours; my God I have never seen so much storage, that must have cost a million." Lance said, "Seven point three million, wrote it off for infrastructure, you see we own the island, well most of it." Mark said, "There is one place for sale, I was going to take a good look at it but I was disrupted by all of this."

Lance asked, "Alex, are you there?" Lance's phone turned on and Alex came up on the screen, he said, "You have to go through customs, we cannot risk you blowing your cover, this is real they are hunting you." Lance said, "That's nice, could you put a hold on a place on Niihau, Mark wants to look at it." Alex said, "That's an easy one, sure." Lance said, "Now please, I am sure you are doing a dozen things at a time." Alex said, "Done, just transferred a hundred grand out of his account to hold it, he still will have to go in front of the council that is to be expected, on the island there is a lot of politics." Lance said, "Thanks."

Mark asked, "How is everything going with your sister Rose?" Alex said, "That is screen five, I have lost Rose, and Patty Bottom. Brent is out in the swamp, what the hell is he doing out there? I have no clue but I have someone looking for him I turned on his tracker and it is still running, Patty's is not working someone is jamming it, something is wrong here."

Mark said, "Crap they got the girls; someone must have checked in, abort the landing." Lance said, "Screw that, we have to find them." Mark said, "Now they know where the girls were, and they are hunting you, do not land." Lance said, "This is my sister, you don't understand, Alex." Lance held out his phone and Alex appeared, Lance said, "I need a flight to Chicago, and then back home booked it a month ago." Alex said, "Roger that, you have to get your butt over here, we have some major work to do, I am calling in favors." Lance said, "I got the tickets, thank you." Alex said, "I have sent you an attachment showing the dis-appearance of the girls and Bent, they just disappear, I have gone through it frame for frame once they stepped through the door they are gone."

Lance opened it and held out his phone so Mark could watch the three of them walking down the street when an old lady waved them into her shop; it was a palm reading place, then nothing. Mark said, "Gas, did you see the seal on the door, and the old lady was turned but you could see her movement she was putting on a mask." Alex said, "Your right, how did I miss that." Lance asked, "When is the last time you slept?" Mark asked, "Do you think they are still there?"

Alex said, "We know Brent is in the swamp not moving and does not have a heartbeat, here we go monitor nine, he has a bag duct taped on his head." Mark said, "Good, that means the girls are alive." Lance cocked his head and said, "Good how the hell is this good, oh you are right if they would have killed them, they would have dumped them together." Mark asked, "This is a satellite feed how long can you watch it, they had to move the bodies." Alex said, "Nothing came out, nobody went in." Lance handed Mark the phone and said, "I have to land this thing figure this out."

Mark asked, "Alex can you zoom out, I want to see the whole complex, where is the loading dock?" Alex said, "This is the French quarter, it was built in 1718, it was built in the Military-style grid of twenty-seven square blocks by Jean Baptiste, and it was called Vieux Carre, and still is today." Mark said, "There is the delivery truck, it pulled under the roof of that building follow the truck." Alex said, "We are going to lose the feed, no wait there they are, the two girls are being loaded into a van, see they are handcuffed and walking that is a good sign."

Mark said, "And here comes a body, and he does have a bag tapped around his neck, into a Jeep he goes."

Alex said, "He was dumped deep in the bayou, I have the plate number from the van the girls were in, it went to a private airstrip, and we are going to lose them there." Lance said, "Damn, well I will see you in eleven hours, have something for me, are your parents home?" Alex asked, "Where are my parents? The CIA had them picked up, oh it doesn't matter the military will treat them nice." Lance said, "That is what got him house arrest, he was trying to put a E.M.P. in a stinger missile, they were just too small, I am sure we can do it but this one had to prove itself, and it did." Mark asked, "Now what?" Lance said, "We sell the patent to the highest bidder." Mark said, "No what are you going to do about the girls." Lance said, "We will find them and rescue them." Mark said, "I am going to New York and regroup; we don't have a clue where they were taken, and I don't know who I can trust."

Lance said, "We will share an Uber, from the airport, I have a long day ahead of me." They just made small talk. Lance asked, "So when are you going to get down and check out that retirement cottage?" Mark said, "I thought it was just over three thousand square feet, that's no cottage, a villa maybe." Lance said, "It's a house on a volcanic island, there are a couple of small farms on the other side of the island, they are ran by retired people also, nothing big vegetables mostly, everything else comes from the big island." Mark asked, "How about meat, and dairy products?"

Lance said, "There is a large freezer at the port, every landowner has a space in it, you put in an order and it is filled and loaded into your little cage, there are strict rules, everything is dated as it is put in there." Mark asked, "How do you know this." Lance said, "I am a landowner; I get all the minutes of the meetings." Mark asked, "You own a house there; I thought it was a retirement community no kids allowed."

Lance said, "Did I say I have a house there? I said land. We own the island, the server, and the power generator, so we make a small profit, and it will take about fifty years to break even." Mark asked, "What kind of maintenance fee is there?" Lance said, "It's not a lake community or anything like that; you can't let the property get run down if you make any changes you have to go in front of the council to add anything, like garages, and fences, stuff like that." Mark asked, "I was talking about grounds keepers, maid service." Lance said, "They have that and they are all cleared, wait now we have this Specter thing they will all be studied, the security is top shelf we can look at every call that has been set to the island and everyone that has left." Mark said, "Now that is the first downside to the place." Lance said, "Oh the security does not monitor your calls. I mean it has the capability of doing it, we are going to have to find the leaks and seal them."

Lance sat the plane down nice and easy, as soon as it stopped. Lance's phone dinged and a van came out to the plane. Lance said, "Things have changed again, I have to shake a leg to meet my flight, your luggage will meet you in New York, the agency had your room packed in Jamaica, mine they found here in New Orleans."

Mark said, "Well that is good, one time I lost my luggage for a month, and I had evidence of a case I was on, if you look at it there are thousands of pieces of luggage getting moved around, I don't know how they keep it straight." Lance said, "The power of computers, it is amazing what they can do, and we tried writing code, getting all the magnetic tags, all the airports have to have the same software, it is a huge task, if we could have sold our idea it would have brought in a hundred million dollars." Mark said, "We need to go through customs." Lance said, "They are in the van, and they will check out the plane, after we are gone, so make sure everything is off the plane."

Lance opened the door stepped down to the pontoon and went to the van handed off his briefcase raised his arms and a man searched him, to his surprise there was a hundred-dollar bill in his hand. Lance said, "Just a tip, thank you for driving me to my next flight, I am in a hurry." Mark stepped over and held up his hands and asked, Lance "Do you do this often?" Lance said, "More than you would think, I fly directly into some of these poor countries, and they still want to know what you are bringing in."

The man said, "You are clean, you can go I am going to give your plane the once over." Lance said, "Please do, we have a pilot from our charity coming to pick it up." Mark asked, "Now the charity, it is serving the jungle people?" Lance smiled and said, "Mostly the Amazon basin, we are trying to protect the rainforest, so first you have to protect the people, we have built schools and bringing work into the area, if they can make a living they will not log off the place, a big thing is they are clearing so much forest to grow crops and raise beef and soybeans, the almighty dollar is killing the world you know."

The man patting down Mark asked, "Where is your luggage, and are we dropping you off at your flight?" Mark said, "My luggage should be catching up to me in New York I hope, and no I have two hours before my flight so just drop me off at Delta, terminal." Lance said, "This is going to be a long day, let's roll I have a plane to catch."

Chapter Fourteen: Off to Greece

Lance got into the van followed by Mark they went to Lance's gate, Lance said to Mark as he got out, "If you learn anything you call me," Mark said, "you do the same, this is time sensitive, the quicker this gets wrapped up the better." Lance headed for a staircase he got to the top to find a large group of people waiting for the plane to start loading. He headed for the bathroom, it was a long flight and he would rather use airport facilities then the one on the plane.

Just as he entered the bathroom they announced his flight was boarding. Lance got in line and boarded the plane and was seated and asked, the guy next to him, "So how long is the layover in Detroit?" He smiled and said, "Depends where you are going, I am headed for New York, it's a three-hour layover." Lance said, "I suppose I will look it up, hey it's only an hour, thank God." Lance got a glass of merlot as soon as he got into the air; he tipped the stewardess twenty bucks that got him attention through the trip. Alex texted him, his flight was just changed, he was headed for Germany. Lance rolled his eyes and got a shot of Royal Crown, as his plane tickets popped up on his phone, he now was heading for Greece.

Alex called and said, "Your luggage is on the plane, get your bag and get over to the International, fly to Munich, there you have a three-hour layover and then to Athens, I will have everything worked out, I am coming to the party." Lance asked, "Are you sure this is where they took Rose and Patty." Alex said, "That picture of the spring lock, I followed the manufacture, they had a large order sent to an island off of Greece, there I saw a plane unload the girls yesterday." Lance asked, "What airport?" Alex said, "Kalamata, then to Milos, from there is a small volcanic island they took a ship to, I have been doing some digging and they must be making a zoo on the island, they are sending a ton of animals there."

Lance said, "Now if I am remembering this right there are like six thousand islands off of Greece and only like two hundred are inhabited." Alex said, "Two hundred and twenty-seven, and this is a small one, they have a herd of a hundred cows grazing in a pasture, and they keep getting shipments, so they are feeding them to something." Lance asked, "Jurassic Park, do you think someone is trying to bring the dinosaurs back again?" Alex said, "I have someone meeting you at the airport, he will have the code word braunschweiger."

Lance said, "By the way did you get the liver pate sent from Usingers out of Milwaukee." Alex said, "And it is very good, damn near ate the whole thing, we are going silent mode for a while, I have more going on right now that you could believe." Lance said, "Ok I am going to Detroit, then to Chicago, overseas to Munich Germany, how long of a flight is that?" Alex said, "Pick up a book in the airport, it is a fourteen-hour flight." Lance asked, "First class." Alex chuckled and said, "Of course, I know how you like flying with the cattle." Lance got to Detroit, found his flight and had a burger and a beer, he was still Henry Rose, it was a quick flight to Chicago just over an hour.

He landed in Chicago and went to a bookstore and quickly bought a book, then headed down to get his luggage. He grabbed his suitcase and headed for the door, looking for the shuttle to the international side. He asked, "How long does it take to get to terminal five?" The girl said, "Once you get on the shuttle twenty to thirty minutes." Lance said, "Thanks." He headed for the nearest cab, "The driver opened the trunk Lance lifted the suitcase and dropped it in and said, "Terminal five and step on it." He pulled a hundred off his money clip and handed it to the man. He smiled and said, "Yes sir, please put on your seat belts."

Lance said, "Just hurry please, and don't get pulled over." The driver said, "I do this for a living, terminal five is a whole different airport, it isn't that far, I can do it in ten minutes without traffic, and doing sixty," he was weaving through the traffic, Lance thought he was going to take the sidewalk to get around a slow driver. He pulled in and said, "Thirteen minutes, not bad at all, I will have to time myself next time there isn't any traffic." Lance said, "Thank you so much, now if I can get through security." The driver said, "They now have buses that take you airside, so you don't have to go through security again." Lance said, "I have time against me; I have to hurry to sit for fourteen hours." The driver handed him his suitcase and said, "You had better hall ass; a shuttle is coming."

Lance quickly walked to the door went in, got his ticket and handed off his bag at the counter and went to security, twenty minutes he was looking for his flight, once he found it they were already loading. Lance got in line and scanned his ticket and got on the plane, he slid his briefcase under his seat and looked at the woman he was sitting with and said, as he sat down, "You know my briefcase will not fit under the seats in the back, they have shortened and narrowed the seats so much."

She said, "It is all about money, now we are not going to talk all the way to Greece, I have work to do." Lance said, "Don't worry about me, I am married," he showed her the ring on his finger, he noticed a seam was starting to show on his wrist. They got up to cruising altitude and Lance slipped the flight attendant a fifty, and said, "Let's make this a good flight and start with a Royal Crown Manhattan." He pulled out his briefcase and put a marker in his shirt pocket and pulled out a book, then put the briefcase back under the seat then he started to read the book. The woman next to him said, "Fairy Sorcery and the Devil, that's interesting." Lance said, "It is different, a race of fairy that has been enslaved, he gets touched by God and given power that he is learning, they bring back Merlin in this story he is an old magician, and the fairy dust is what brings back his youth, he talks about when he was a kid and Bobba-Yaga was his teacher, and how he was saved from the dragons that ate everyone in his village. I am almost done with it, I bought Fairy Sorcery and the Greek Gods, after that the book is Fairies Sorcery and the Titians, it is a trilogy, I hope they have that for the ride home."

The woman asked, "So why are you going to Greece?" Lance rolled his eyes and asked, "Why are you talking to me? This is my plan I read for a couple of hours, have a couple of drinks, take a nap, stand up walk around, work for a hour read more of my book have a couple of drinks and take another nap." The woman asked, "When you are done with the book do you mind if I look at it." Lance said, "No that is fine."

He got up and went to the bathroom, he sat down and pulled out the marker it was liquid flesh he put it on the seam of his hand and blended it in, then stood and looked into the mirror, straightened out one ear and blended the makeup around one eye, he felt the Velcro seam up the back of his neck, it was covered by the hair of the mask. He went back to his seat, stopping and ordering another Manhattan. He sat down finished his book and handed it to the woman next to him and put on a sleep mask, and noise canceling ear buds, and went right to sleep. He woke when they were serving dinner; he had a salad, smoked duck, and an ice-cream sundae.

He pulled up the mission on his laptop and found out what Alex had in plan for him. He had an invitation to a sporting event, with a million dollar buy in. There wasn't much of a description of what it was, just what dock and what time. He went to the research and watched people load onto the ferry; they were dressed a little more than business casual, suit and a tie, some in tuxes. Women were all in dresses, some in evening wear. The man at the dock checked the briefcases, he zoomed in and you could see the stacks of money. He noticed lights flashing in the doorway of the ferry, it was a scanner, as soon as someone walked through a light flashed either red or green.

Chapter Fifteen: To the Arena

He went to Germany then to Athens in Kalamat. He went through customs and got his luggage and headed to his next flight to Milos. Most people who worked there spoke Greek which made it interesting; this was a smaller airport when he got off and went down to get his luggage a man stood holding a sign saying "Henry Rose." Lance walked over and asked, "Are you looking for Henry Rose?" The man said, "Well yes I am." Lance said, "Interesting, I saw him earlier." The man said, "Braunschweiger." Lance smiled and said, "I am Henry, so you are my ride then."

He held out his hand and said, "I am Luke Papadopoulos." Lance shook his hand and said, "Nice to meet you, Andrew Brown, grew up in Atlanta, you are agent 159." Luke said, "God I hate computers; I was scrubbed from the data base." Lance smiled and said, "I have good facial recognition software, and I will make a note of scrubbing your file, did you get the package." He said, "Yes sir, and where will you be staying?" Lance smiled and said, "They are keeping you in the dark, I like that," he said and took his suitcase off the carousel.

Luke said, "It is amazing how many bags are stolen in baggage claim, tens of thousands of bags go through an airport a day." Lance said, "That is why you buy the good bags that have GPS, if I can't find my bag, I just call it and ask where it is." Luke said, "Really, that beat up thing is high tec." Lance smiled and said, "Ok to the Volcano Suites hotel, it is like three miles away, I can get dressed."

They got into the car Lance asked, "Did you get the money?" Luke smiled and said, "This is the first time I have seen a million dollars in cash." Lance said, "You have a southern accent." Luke said, "I have been here working on a case for almost two years." Lance said, "I know, we hacked into the CIA data base, this job is a big one, you can come up to my room, we have an hour and a half before getting on the ferry at Polonia Port; it is a half hour drive, so we have to shake a leg." They got to the room Lance asked, "Do you have a gun?" Luke said, "Well yeah I am carrying a million dollars." Lance said, "Good I am going to need it; you are not coming on the ferry." Luke looked sad he was going to miss the action. Lance said, "This is the way it works only the investors go to the island."

Luke asked, "So what are you investing in?" Lance said, "This is a very sensitive mission, a life and death one, there are many players, your job is to get me to the ferry with the million bucks, it doesn't have a tracker does it." Luke said, "No I don't think so." Lance raised an eyebrow and asked, "You didn't scan it did you?" Luke said, "Was I supposed to?"

Lance took out his tux and hung it running a bar across it taking out the wrinkles and, took out the shoes polishing them with his socks. Luke said, "It's a black-tie thing." Lance said, "Yes what a pain in the ass, people act differently when they are dressed," Lance took off his shirt revealing the mask and where his hands start showing Luke this wasn't who he was." Luke said, "Those are fresh scars on your back."

Lance asked, "How do they look, are they healing?" Luke said, "It looks good no infection." Lance turned and smiled as he said, "I was questioned for a few days, good times," he went in the bathroom and touched up his makeup, blending in everything. Luke said, "You are good at that." Lance said, "I did theater, for a couple of semesters, there was this girl I wanted to get close to."

Luke said, "Been there." Lance said, "She was selling heroin to pay for college, took her down and her dealer, and his dealer, got an A in extra credit." Luke asked, as he gave Lance his gun, "Am I ever going to see this again." Lance smiled as he took the gun, "I highly doubt it, a Springfield APC 45 I thought you were CIA not FBI, oh I need your phone number and here is a key to the hotel room, you might have to ship my suitcase to me." Luke said, "I just am not a fan of 9mm, I want stopping power, when I shoot somebody, I only want to do it once." Lance smiled "Good choice, do you have another clip?" Luke said, "Not with me this was just a pickup and delivery."

Lance said, "Let's go, we can't be late, and we can't be too early." They got to the port and the ferry was sitting there. Lance said, "You are to walk me to the security guards, and hand over the money, they are going to scan the money and me for bugs at least they should." Luke asked, "Have you done this before?" Lance looked at him with a bit of fear in his eyes and said, "No never, this has to work there are lives on the line, once I get through security get out of here, I will call you if I need you." Luke said, "A car just pulled up."

Lance said, "Ok, shall we walk right behind them it is Amon Salah Shah from the Middle East, a very deadly man." Luke got out and took the small aluminum suitcase he caught up to Lance, and said, "You know I thought a million dollars would weigh a lot more." Lance said, "A million dollars in hundreds weighs around seventeen pounds, now if it was in twenties, it would weigh around 1.1 tons, and in pennies it would weigh 281 tons, so just be glad it is in hundreds."

The shah's group of five walked down the pier, one man was out front and the rest followed back a few feet, once they got to the security the front man stopped short and another stepped out followed by a man holding a large briefcase. Security ran a wand over the man and the case, then opened the case to check the cash. The man took the case and headed for the ferry. Lance walked up to the security, and Luke handed off the briefcase. Lance flashed the invitation, they ran the wand over him, he took the briefcase and headed to the ferry without saying a word.

He got to the ferry they were handing out champagne, he held up his hand to refuse it, and he started to scan the ship, he would double blink and, in his glasses, it would show him who the person was what he did for a living, these were the bad of the bad, all multimillionaires, everything was uploaded to a server and transferred to his supercomputer. His phone was searching for hackers, he was sure he wasn't the only one checking out the crowd. He noticed a senator, one of the Royal families of Austria, two congressmen, the party chairman, he knew some of the people personally, but nobody knew him, Henry Rose was a fictional figure, made up just so Lance and Alex could slip off the grid. Every person on the ferry had a small suitcase or large briefcase, so there was at least fifty million on the ferry. It was an hour cruise, Lance made small talk to people he did not know, mostly kept to himself and listened to the conversations.

The ferry docked and as everyone stepped off the ship they walked between six different dogs then through a scanner. Lance had Luke's 45 strapped to his ankle, he noticed the bulge under a few of the men's arms and they walked right through, he smiled knowing they were looking for bombs and chemical weapons. They walked to an auto walk, a large man said to him, "I love these things." Lance said, with power in his voice "It was patented back in 1955 by Otis Elevator they called it a Trav-O-Lator, everyone calls it an auto walk." The big man said with a Russian accent, "I am Boris Smirnoff."

Lance said, "I am Henry Rose; I am not here to make friends." Boris said, "The meetings are killers, but the entertainment is good, no?" Lance watched how this worked, everyone stood in a line as their cash was weighed, it was all American hundred-dollar bills, and one guy pulled two stacks out of his suit jacket and handed it to the man. The man behind him said, "Now let's see if they leave him live, you don't cheat Specter."

Lance was casing the place, there were cameras everywhere, and all the guards were carrying mac tens. Lance got up to the counter and handed the small suitcase to the man, the man handed him a card, with a I-pad and said, "There is a million on the card, if you would swipe it please, this is what you will be placing bets on." Lance swiped the card and it showed a one and six zeros, he just nodded to the man, turned and followed the other men. As he got closer to the doors he could smell animals, once he entered the room, he could see it was a small arena it looked like it would hold a thousand people. A waitress came around and took drink orders and served hors d'oeuvres, his I-pad lite with a lion and a guy in a suit, two guards grabbed the guy that tried to cheat the count of the million, was dragged down toward the arena floor, the walls were about twelve feet high so nothing could jump into the seated area.

One guy next to Lance said, "I wonder what Senior Thomas did." Lance smiled and said, "He tried to skim a few thousand off his million buy in." The man said, "I know this lion, see the left ear was cut off, and the scare on the neck, he is a mean one, gained a little weight thou he was 400 pounds now he is 420, I give Thomas two minutes fifteen seconds." Lance studied the I-pad it told the weight and age of the lion and the man, he looked at all the exits and looked up to see his sister Rose with a white haired guy holding a white cat, he looked back at his sister she was sitting in a chair in front of the window to watch the games.

He was studying the theater when he saw Mark he was almost straight across on the other side of the Arena, right above him was a door to the glass room Rose was in. There was a timer counting down on the I-pad, Lance picked the lion to win, clicked on $50,000 with no time limits. The timer ran out and a lion popped up from a trap door, it roared echoing in the arena. The guy turned white as a sheet, he lifted a sword, the lion walked slowly around him, the timer was running. The man in front of Lance yelled, "Kill him."

Lance knew he was taking to the lion, the lion snarled and could sense the fear in him and rushed him batting away the sword and sinking his large teeth into his neck and head, he shook the man like a ragdoll. The crowd cheered blood shot out onto the sand, the lion had a paw on him and was ripping off his shirt. The man next to him calmed down and said, "Did you see that? Two minutes and fifteen seconds, I won big time," then he said, in a quieter voice, "It is ok to win, just not too much the house doesn't like that, and I am allergic to cats."

Lance said, "I got you, so how much is too much." The man said, "Watch this sometimes it doesn't go well." About twenty men with shields and long cattle prods came out of gated door and lined up to drive the lion back, they walked shoulder to shoulder. Lance asked, "What happens if the cat gets around them?" The man said, "That's what makes it interesting." The lion looked at them then the other way to a door with a hind quarter of a cow hanging there, the cat turned and slowly walked into the doorway and the gate dropped and the cat was lowered underground.

Lance asked, "Have you ever been under the floor of the arena that must be something." The man said, "No and I don't know anyone that has, that's for the workers, and they do go thru a few of those, I bet ten grand three workers die today." Lance said, "Really? I would think they would be more careful." The man said, "Some of the Gladiators are animals, they are kept alive just to fight."

Lance got up and made his way to the bottom he looked up at Rose; she was watching him, he looked away quickly and watched the next match, a man walked out carrying a sword, he was doing some stretching when two men road in on horseback carrying spears, they both had numbers on them. Lance watched for a few seconds looked at his I-pad and chose one of the horsemen, $30,000 bet then the timer went to zero and a gong was hit, one man charged the man straight on with his spear pointed at him.

The man on the ground jumped to the other side of the horse and plunged the sword into the horse right behind the front shoulder right to the hilt piercing the other side, putting the sword right through the heart, he pulled out the sword it was coated with deep red blood and it shot out of both sides of the horse with every beat of the heart. The rider swung the spear over the horse to the other side and the man stepped in close and stuck him in the leg. The horse took one last leap, crumbling up when it hit the ground it laid there kicking pinning its rider to the ground. The man quickly focused on the other horseman, this one was much more careful not to get to close, he circled the man, then trotted away, turned and came in at a full gallop making sure he didn't come to close, the man on the ground deflected the spear.

The horseman turned and took another run, the man crouched to make a smaller target, he leaped toward the oncoming horse the horseman made the adjustment and speared him through the stomach, losing his spear. He got off the horse and pulled out a sword. The speared man was trying to run the spear through him to get free, his hands were covered with blood, and he couldn't pull free of the spear. The horseman stepped over to him and with one mighty swing of the sword the guy's head came right off and rolled on the sand, he walked over and bent down picked up the head he walked around the arena holding up the head. The crowd were on their feet, cheering him on. Lance looked down at his I-pad and shook his head he had picked the wrong one. The Gladiator held up the head and his sword looking up to the man in the glass. The man gave a slight bow. Rose was crying, she didn't want to watch this.

Lance paid a guard to let him see the operation under the floor, there were cages with bears, lions, tigers, and Gladiators all in cells. He studied the floor above some of the cages, they had the quick release Alex had patented, and large springs under the cage; that is how they could just pop in an animal in the arena. He walked by a cage, there was Patty Bottom, she was wearing a leopard skin, and that was it. She stared at him, Lance shook his head, and turned away asking the guide how everything worked, a man was poking a large grizzly bear, the bear was really pissed off, it was snarling, swatting at the spear. A man slowly rose with his cage into the arena. Lance looked down at his I-pad and picked the bear to win and this time he scrolled to five minutes and put in a bid for a hundred grand. The man said, "You have to go; you have a minute before we release the bear."

Lance said, "This is a great setup, so you get the orders and everything is done right at the computer, just a touch of a key." The man said, "That's pretty much it, you had better go." Lance got up to the stands just as the bear was popped into the arena, it stood for a minute looking at the crowd, then finding the man with a small axe. Lance gave a small wave to Mark, then thumbs up sign, everyone was watching the fight Lance was programming his three darts with his phone, and making it look like he was watching the bear tear the man apart, he knew if he was caught on his phone he would be in the ring. The men came out to drive the bear back into a cage, the bear had nothing to do with this, he came right at them, then poof he was gone, a trap door opened and there was a clean spot on the floor.

The next contestant was Patty; she was slowly raised onto the arena floor, there was some jeering, and she had a shield and a sword. Lance took a couple of steps to the door going under the floor, he turned and fired the darts, one went to the door above Mark, the other went to a beam that was holding the roof, and the third went to the entrance of the cleanup crew. The blast of each dart was deafening, the door above Mark blew right off the hinges, the doorway to the arena was a big steel bar door, the dart hit the keypad next to it. The one that went into the rafters to the beam hit and a few smaller beams fell but the roof held. Then all hell broke loose, you could see holes being shot through the roof from the outside, parts of the steel roof were falling to the arena, and troops were dropping in.

Mark ran for the door; the man that was holding Rose ran across the room to an elevator. Mark was right behind him waiting for the elevator to come back up, he cleared the room and left Rose chained to the chair. He went down three stories to a large empty room, it had a submarine docking station, he carefully walked around the room making sure the man was not hiding then he waited for the elevator to open to go back up.

Lance ran to the door going under the floor to stop whatever they were sending up to battle Patty. He had his 45 in his hand and head shot the guard outside the door and grabbed his Mac ten and three clips while the man was flopping around from nerves. He ran down the staircase and fired on the guy at the computer; he ran his hand across all the switches and hit a button sending all the cages up. Lance damn near cut him in half with the Mac, he looked and there was no way to get up to the arena, he ran back to the door to find anarchy, troops were rappelling down from the roof.

Rose was still chained to the chair, and Alex was flying across the arena with a jet pack and two chain sixty, blazing this was a major military action. Lance ran to where Patty was battling with a Gladiator he hung from the edge of the arena and dropped down. Three men unloaded into the huge grizzly taking it to the ground, a huge bull came running by plowing down people. Lance fired one round hitting the Gladiator who was battling Patty in the neck, he screamed as he got to Patty, "We have to go!" He grabbed her arm and pulled towards the wall. He fired his pistol at a large Russian boar, the pig took a hit and kept on going. They got to the wall and Lance pulled her down behind a dead horse. Patty yelled, "Rose!"

Lance said, "Keep your head down, Alex is taking care of it," he looked up to see Alex hovering in front of the glass cutting it with a laser, and flying into the room, he got the jet pack off and went and unchained Rose. He fired his weapon a few times, but it was over rather quickly. Lance stood with his hands in the air, overlooking the carnage, the arena was covered with the bodies of animals and humans, and bodies littered the stands, Lance pulled Patty tight and said, "Everyone in the stands was carrying so they were a threat." She kissed him and pulled back and said, "Your face is falling off." Lance reached around and grabbed his mask from the back seam and slowly pulled it off, she then kissed him again, a long passionate kiss, he closed his eyes and enjoyed the moment." His pocket buzzed, Lance pulled away and answered the call, then texted "I can't hear a damn thing, is everything good?"

Alex gave the thumbs up sign holding Rose tight, with a smile ear to ear. Lance text "Where is Mark?" Just at that moment Mark stepped out of a blank wall behind Alex in the glass room. Alex texted, "Don't move, stay safe, this is going to take a few minutes to lock down." Lance looked at Mark pointing to the jet pack. Every once and a while a gunshot would go off, as the army went thru the wounded animals, and if a wounded man would have a weapon, they put them down.

A man walked over to Lance and said, "The General would like to say something." Lance said, "Yes Sir." The man turned an I-pad to Lance and General Armstrong said, "Good job Lance, your father is safe with us; you can see him as soon as possible." Lance said, "General Armstrong, this is agent Patty Bottom, this has been a shitfest, most of the Specter would rather be killed then to surrender, this is most of the bosses in the world, and the man in charge got away."

The general said, "No he got to a mini sub and was sunk, we are retrieving the body now, this was a very well-orchestrated mission, you do know you are going to have to be debriefed, both of you." Lance smiled and said, "We will write up a report, and get back to you next week," Lance reached out and hit end the man said, "You just hung up on the General, that is not wise."

Lance said, "Don't worry, he is a friend of the family, now I need a ride to my hotel, I need to get cleaned up and you need a shower, who knows where that fur has been." She smiled and asked, "Do you like it?" Lance winked and said, "It would look better on the bedroom floor." He pulled out his phone and texted "Volcano Suites Hotel, it's close to the airport." The sergeant said, "It could be a while before you get a ride; we are in the middle of something." Lance said, "Alex, oh crap, he isn't listening."

Patty asked, "Isn't it his computer that was listening?" Alex texted "What?" Lance smiled and said, to Patty, "You are a smart one." Lance texted back, "I will order a helicopter for a ride." Alex texted "Twenty minutes at the dock, and don't be late." Lance smiled and said, "I wish Rose would give him a chance; he would make a great brother-in-law." Patty said, "She is a lot older isn't she." Lance smiled and said, "She isn't as old as you, she is five years older and you are ten years older than me and I don't have a problem with that, come on we have to get down to the dock, sergeant would you have one of your men escort us to the dock, I would hate to get shot by friendly fire."

Patty wrapped her arm around him and asked, "How did you find us?" Lance smiled and said, "It is a small world, Alex and I patented a hinge that would hold four ton, and open and close in a second, I thought it was for a magical act, not a coliseum, but it did work well." She asked, "Did you have anything to do with all the cages being opened." Lance said, "Nope that was one of the workers, I did shoot at him first, and everything came together so fast." Patty said to the soldier they were following, "I hear the helicopter; we have to move a little faster."

Lance said, "It's an old Russian KA-52, this is a good old helicopter, all the controls are in Russian." Patty asked, "Can you fly a helicopter?" Lance said, "Not only fly we have a patent on a fire copter it still has a few kinks in it that we are working out, I have flown almost every helicopter on the market." They got down and met Alex and Rose, Rose was so happy to see him she threw her arms around him and said, "Ouch, my God I feel like 6 miles of bad road." Lance said, "You and me sister, are you ok?" Rose said, "Other than been beaten, drugged, raped, chained up, not bad." Lance chuckled and said, "Well Alex you were right, this was the place, and those hinges worked flawlessly, are you guys staying at our hotel."

Alex said, "Tonight we are, tomorrow I have a private jet taking us to Washington D.C. we are staying on the governments dime, in a five-star hotel." Rose said, "We have to stop at a pharmacy on the way to the hotel; I need makeup, Band-Aids, ibuprofen, and the day after pill." Patty said, "Oh God I need that; in fact, I would take two." Lance pulled her tight and said, "I am so sorry, what the hell happened to Brent? He was supposed to take care of you, it must have been terrible for you two." Rose sobbed and said, "They gassed us and killed him once I got here, I was kept in the lap of luxury, champagne and caviar." Patty said, "That wasn't where I was staying, I was glad the locked me up in a cage to keep the animals away from me, guys are gross."

They got to their hotel rooms and Lance said, "I hope you don't mind I bought you some clothes, the leopard skin is a turn on but just not for a sit-down meal." Patty looked at a shirt and skirt hanging in the closet, and a pair of jeans and blouse. She smiled and said, "You know, you are a nice guy." Lance said, "We have forty-five minutes then we have to meet Alex and Rose for dinner." Patty asked, "Would you like to take a shower?"

Lance smiled and said, "Sure, and you do know you are going to have two black eyes." Patty pulled him into a hug and kissed him passionately pushing him onto the bed. Lance said, "You are turning me on, but you smell nasty, did you fall in a pile of horse poop." Patty laughed and said, "I thought that was you."

Alex got into the hotel room with Rose she said, "I owe you my life." Alex said, as he took her hand, and stared into her eyes, "I love you, and I have ever since I met you." He pulled her close and kissed her on the cheek." She pulled back and kissed him full on the mouth, a nice slow long kiss. He opened his eyes and said, "This is not going to happen, at least not now, I love you that is why I got two queens." She said, as she kissed him again, "Oh Alex, that just makes me want you more."

Alex said, "I am going to take a quick shower, Lance bought you some clothes, there is so much to do." He went in the bathroom and started the shower and Rose stepped in right behind him and said, "This will not last but at least we have tonight." Alex looked at her and said, "This is a point in time, that I will remember for the rest of my life, I am done hurry up we have to meet Lance downstairs." Rose said, "Really, I stand before you naked and all you think about is food." Alex said, "You are beautiful, I love you, but it is not the time." He shaved and got dressed, brought in the clothes for Rose to wear and said, "You have ten minutes."

When she came out of the bathroom Alex had his phone out, two laptops, his briefcase open with wires sticking out of it, he turned and said, "I have to get home, this is just way to slow to work with." Rose asked, "Can't you interface with your computers at home?" Alex smiled and said, "The government gave me free range, I am cracking open more networks than you can believe, Specter is a web and it runs deep, far reaching the ends of the Earth, we are cleaning up your casino, it will be safe to go back to work, that is what you want to do, right?"

Rose said, "More than ever, I built that show, and to receive the applause it is so gratifying," she messaged his neck and asked, "Are we going down for dinner or would you like to eat it in bed?" Alex finished a sentence stood and looked at her a bit weird and asked, "Eat supper in bed, really is that an option? We are to meet Lancelot, and Miss Patty, well actually her name is Susan Tucker, right now we are calling her Joy-ass, you get it she was Patty Bottom now she is Joyce, Holder." He stood and Rose wrapped her arms around him and said, as she kissed him, "I owe you one, he was talking about putting me in the arena if I didn't do exactly what he said."

He reached down with both hands and cupped her butt lifting her off the ground then gently setting her back down running both up the sides of her backbone slowly and firmly. She pulled away from the kiss and purred "That feels so good." Alex said, "Let's do this, I give you ten years, you will be thirty three, if you are not married, we will get together and have kids, I will do whatever it takes to make you happy." She kissed his neck and worked up to his ear and said, "I am good with that, ten years." He pushed her away and said, "We have a bottle of Dom Perignon 2004 waiting for us."

Lance and Patty were down sipping champagne, when Alex came down. Lance stood as Rose sat. She looked at Lance and said, "Oh my God, Dad is he alright?" Lance smiled and said, "Yes he is fine." Alex said, with a smile, "Your brother blew up the submarine he was on, luckily he didn't kill him." Lance shot him a look and said, "It was a risk we had to take; everything went well we won't see him for a couple of weeks."

Alex said, "Unless he goes to prison, then it might be a couple of decades." Rose looked with her jaw hanging. Lance said, "Boy your just doom and gloom today, when is the last time you slept?" Alex asked, "You mean the whole night that would be the day I found out you were missing, what is that eight days ago?" Lance raised a glass and said, "To the end of a mission, and a start of a new one." Everyone said, before they took a drink, "To the end of the mission." Patty said, "What mission are you starting?"

Lance said, "Taking down Specter, this is going to topple countries, we might be talking war." Rose said, "Come on, war really?" Alex said, "If it is not done correctly, yes we are talking hundreds of thousands of deaths, and here comes our first course, this is the last we talk about this." Rose said to Lance, "In ten years if I am not married and Alex isn't married, we are going to have children together." Lance smiled and asked, "Did he get you to sign the contract?" Rose said, "What contract?" Lance said, "He wrote one five years ago; you would be 33 years old and he would be twenty-seven." Patty said, "You were eleven when you wrote it."

Alex blushed and said to Rose as he stared into her eyes "I told you I have loved you for a long time, but now is not a good time for romance." Rose smiled and said, "At least we have tonight." Lance asked, "Aren't you putting her in protective custody?" Alex said, "No, I am working with the service, and think she can go back to work." Lance shook his head and said, "Your heart is clouding your mind, do not put her at risk." Rose changed the subject and said, "Miss Joy-ass," she grinned as she asked, "What are you going to do now?"

Patty said, "Well we have to write up a report, so we will be working on that together." Lance said, "I have work to do, Alex and I are going to be really busy." Alex said, "Extremely busy, I am free of house arrest." Rose asked, "What happened with Mark Neal?" Lance said, "Come on Rose, he is forty years old." Patty said, "Oh but he is so debonair, and manly." Rose looked at her and raised an eyebrow, and said, "He is a good boy, he saved my life."

Alex said, "That was me, I hacked into the security cameras talked with the Don, oh Tony Breaker at the Luxor, I was the one that kept you safe." Lance said, "I know what you are thinking, yes Alex and I got you the job, but you created the show, you are so much better than you were when you first started." She looked at Alex and asked, "You did that for me?" Lance said, "Don't answer that it could bite you in the ass, yes we might have forced him to hire you, but he does not regret it, that raise you got was all Tony, your shows are sold out. I wonder how it is doing with your understudy?" She snapped her head and stared right into his eyes and said,

"That's right, Sheila is headlining ok I am ready to go back." Alex said, "I am working on that, you need to go and see your doctor, Tony wants a clean book of health, and Mark is in debriefing on his way to D.C. he is going to be busy for a while, and Lance if you would like to bring Patty along that is fine with me." Lance said, "She needs to see a doctor too it has been a hard couple of days."

Meanwhile Mark landed in Washington for his debriefing, he went down to baggage claim and a very nice-looking woman walked over he smiled ear to ear. She said, blushing "James you look rather nice, age is treating you well." He said, "Well Lorraine you are looking very nice, very nice indeed this is not a coincidence is it?" She stepped in close and gave him a hug and whispered in his ear, "You're not going to your debriefing, there is a large price on your head; you will never make your hotel."

He kissed her then whispered, "So what are we going to do." She smiled and said, "I am going to take care of you, here are your tickets." He took the tickets and said, "Hawaii really, man that is a long flight." She smiled and said, "Here comes the luggage, it is a straight flight around nine hours." He said, "I just did ten and a half hours; this is like flying around the world." She looked up at him and said, "Awe is the baby whining, suck it up buttercup." Mark pulled a card from his wallet and said, "Mark Neal, Private Eye, and that is a good number." She took it and said, "We don't have much time, I am Misty Flex, fashion buyer." He said, "And here is mine," he took off a suitcase and garment bag. She said, "I will take the suitcase, follow me."

He said, "Sure whatever you say," he pulled out the handle and she took it and power walked to immigration and customs, it took an hour to get onto the bus to the domestic side of the airport and checked his luggage, Misty kept looking around and said, "If they were going to take you out this is where they would have a chance to do it." Mark smiled and said, "No airports have too many cameras, the cab ride to the hotel, or at the hotel, so how much is on my head?" She smiled and said, "A half million, I thought about it myself sense you bought the only property for sale on the island."

Mark chuckled and said, "So that's it, you want my house." Misty said, "I have been inquiring about it and poof you made a down payment, and I hear you are looking for a wife, so here I am." Mark said, "Really what makes you sure I would marry you?" She laughed and said, "I am not proposing, I am saving your life, we do have a history those three weeks in Brazil, that weekend in Paris." Mark said, "Toronto, London, and Moscow." She looked at him and said, "We never worked together in Moscow." Mark said, "No but I watched every move you made, for two weeks and was wishing I was with you." She rolled her eyes up to meet his and said, "That's cute, this just might work, I need a place to stay for a while, you just don't know who to trust."

They got to the gate to their flight he said, "You know I have to get some clothes, I have been living out of my suitcase for four weeks now." Misty said, "I have that taken care of we did a 1651 upon your death everything in your apartment was packed, put on a truck and put into storage." He said, "Oh no, that sucks I have had to retrieve my stuff once before and that is a pain in the ass." Misty smiled and said, "So everything went into a truck, and then went to a U-Haul, from there it went to a pod, by the way you have nice stuff, and it was packed very well, it should be in Hawaii by the time we get there." Mark said, "Wow you have planned this for a while." Misty said, "No you have some friends in high places, time to board."

They were on board the plane for nine hours they talked Mark was feeling her out and asking questions like if she gardened, or if she can cook, what she wants to do for the rest of her life, if there were anything she would like to do, places to go, who she knew on the island, is she going to live out of her suitcase?" She smiled and said, "Everything I own is on its way to your house, I have talked with Pierce and Keely and they said, if it doesn't work out, I can live in their guest house." Mark said, "You have this all figured out."

She said, "We will work out the details when we get there, there has to be rules, and I need my space." Mark said, "Well this should be fun the house is mine before you moved in." She looked at him and said, "You're thinking divorce before we are married." Mark said, "So you want to be Misty Neal?" She said, "No whoever gives out the names should be shot, Misty sounds like a hooker's name, how about Juliet and you can be my Romeo."

They landed on Hawaii Mark said, "I will call for a helicopter." She said, "Just follow me." They went down to the baggage claim they got their luggage and she said, see that man with the bright Hawaiian shirt going to the bathroom follow him, Mark followed him into the bathroom the man took off his shirt and said, "So 666 you're retiring?" Mark took off his shirt and handed it to him, and said, "Ah 552 so you're my diversion? You look the part." He put on a pair of glasses that looked like Mark's and said, "You sure have stirred up a hornets' nest, trust no one, and I do mean no one the office is tearing itself apart," he handed Mark a bright yellow pamphlet he pulled out of his back pocket. Mark smiled and looked at it, it was Hertz rent a car he put it in his back pocket, and said, "Thanks, this is pretty elaborate."

He smiled and said, "You have a high price on your head, Specter wants you gone, now slouch you are to be shorter on the way out." Mark bent at the knees and hunched his back he looked a good six inches shorter he went to Misty she was talking to a woman when Mark walked up to the other woman, she winked at him. The man that looked like Mark came out and walked up to Misty and she left for the restroom followed by the girl Mark was chatting with. When they got into the restroom, they stepped into a stall together. The woman took off her hat and wig and handed it to Misty, then she shook out her long red hair.

Misty flipped her hair and put on the black wig and tucked any red sowing under it then put on the hat. The woman handed her some eye makeup and took her dark shadow off. Misty kicked off her shoes and exchanged them with her flip-flops then changed shirts. Misty gave the girl a bright lipstick, she put it on and said, "Ok we are good to go." They left the bathroom Misty walked up to Mark and the girl that looked like her went over to Mark's decoy. She hugged Mark and said, "We have to get some distance from those two, they are flying to Seattle renting a car and disappearing in Oregon."

They stepped outside got a taxi and went to the docks, she said, "There is a no-fly zone over the island now, and you can only dock in the dock area, it is pretty much on lock down." They got onto a ship that was heading to the island with a month's supply of food. Misty said, "I had Pierce order what we need for a month, there is a small store on the other side of the island but that has very little and the mark it up is a hundred percent." Mark said, "Well this should be interesting the house had no furniture, where are we going to sleep?"

Misty said, "At Keely's guest house of course, I figure it will take a week to get everything the way we want it, I think we will grow together. I like being with you." Mark kissed her forehead and said, "I guess we have to, but this is not the way I planned it." She smiled and said, "I figure it will cool down in a year or two, let's enjoy it while we are in paradise."

The End

www.ingramcontent.com/pod-product-compliance
Lightning Source LLC
Chambersburg PA
CBHW070834160726
48004CB00001B/381

9798887294339